CW01217512

The Orphan Sniper

By J M Trotter

Copyright © 2012 J M Trotter

All rights reserved

ISBN-13: 978-1478192923

ISBN-10: 1478192925

The characters and events portrayed in this novel are entirely fictitious. Any resemblance between them and actual individuals or events is coincidental, not intended and should not be inferred.

For Lesley, Louise and Ben

Extract from a letter written by Heinrich Himmler to The German Minister of Armaments and War Production, Albert Speer in World War 2.

Dear Party Member Speer,

Perhaps you have already heard that I'm encouraging and accelerating the sharpshooting training in the Grenadier Divisions. We have already attained outstanding results. I have initiated a contest between all divisions of the army and the SS that are under my command. With the 50th confirmed sharpshooter hit – that is, when he has virtually eliminated a Soviet Infantry Company – each man receives a wristwatch from me and reports to my Field Headquarters. With the 100th hit, he receives a hunting rifle and with the 150th, he is invited by me to go hunting to shoot a stag or chamois buck.

Heinrich Himmler

The Caribbean - Tortola

Wednesday 23rd February 1966

Schedule for the Opening of The Queen Elizabeth Bridge

12.10pm   The Royal party will arrive at the bridge.

The Member for Trade and Production will present The Queen with a pair of scissors and invite Her Majesty to cut a tape across the bridge entrance. Her Majesty and His Royal Highness will walk across the bridge.

12.15pm   The Royal car will draw up on the Beef Island side of the bridge. The Queen and The Duke of Edinburgh will enter and drive across Beef Island.

At 12.12pm, Gunter pulled the trigger.

1

The Caribbean - Tortola

Wednesday 06.00 - 16th February 1966

Snoopy went to sleep before the sun moved across the tiled floor to The Doctor's feet wearing twenty thousand mile shoes made from car tires. She was tired from the race. The first corner was sharp and The Doctor burned off rubber hanging a left. Squealing until the tread bit and he picked up speed heading for the Maserati, accelerating into the last bend and taking it wide enough to graze the wall on the right. He entered the final straight in a gentle drift and in a few seconds, the first Maserati would be history. With a last scream of rubber, he came to a stop sideways to the fridge and Snoopy scrabbled after him round the corner searching for the same control the low profile tyres gave her master. Four paws scratching at the polished surface, desperate for a grip on the tiles then smacking into the wall with a furry thud to bounce straight again and celebrate the arrival of dawn skidding on her backside ready for a Maserati. A bottle of gin mixed with a bottle of red wine equals a Maserati. The Doctor's cocktail.

'One for me and one for my baby. Do you want a bowl or a glass Snoops?' There was no reply, 'a bowl isn't so messy.' The Doctor poured

red liquid into a fruit bowl and put it on the floor and the dog drank with her tail rigid.

'Not too quick. Watch me,' he took delicate sips of the Maserati to demonstrate but the dog ignored him and finished her bowl.

'It's not good manners to win every time. I get more than you, but you're smaller.'

The dog raised her head from the empty bowl, 'woof.'

'Oh, all right...just one more,' and he ladled a second Maserati from the punch bowl, 'don't gulp this.'

The dog looked at The Doctor towering above and he seemed to grow taller as the alcohol took effect. She liked the morning race to the fridge and slept while he shaved and got ready to go down the drive for a proper drink at the bar. The other man in the house slept for a long time in the mornings and didn't drink the Maserati for breakfast. Perhaps he was sick. She turned her head towards his bedroom door.

'Keeping a weather eye out for our soldier Snoops,' said The Doctor, 'trouble is the Chief sent Jayce as his infantryman but he's my nephew. Got the looks for a honeytrap. Bit of a temperamental fellow mind you. I said to him "can't be certain we've found our war criminal," but the boy wants to get into action and make a name for himself. The Chief has gone all impatient and says the visit of The Queen next Wednesday is a marker. We need to get the job done when security is high. Problem is Snoops, there are too many bloody unknowns for my taste. Have we got the right German...can Jayce pull it off?' He swallowed the last of his drink, 'and who knows who is who? Plenty of deceit around Snoops. People like Henry who arrived the same time as me on the island. Bit of a coincidence. Probably means nothing but the old security nerves jangle and the antenna twitches.'

The Doctor stared at the guest bedroom and imagined Jayce the assassin, sleeping inside. He dipped his glass into the mixture of red wine and gin. An early sharpener that sped like a Maserati through his system and blasted the haze of sleep to life.

    'One for the road Snoops. Today is surgery time and we need Maseratis to face the operating theatre.'

The Doctor had a rule that when daylight reached his feet at the fridge, night ended, day began and he must leave. That was the rule and there was no way a man of honour could break it. But he refused to look at the creeping dawn, averted his eye from the light, and took another sip. Luxuriating in the final minutes of darkness and fixed his eyes on his shoes, which grew enormous with concentration. Shoes made from a white walled car tyre. The sole and heel were cut from black rubber tread and white cross straps from the tire wall. They were a gift from a friend in South Africa and a little worn but still good for twenty thousand miles.

Which was how far he'd like to run away from the fucking daylight that finally made it to his right foot, and he downed the Maserati in a gulp. Creative arithmetic meant he'd not taken a drink today and could go to the bar at the end of the drive with an easy conscience.

'Follow me Snoops,' The Doctor changed into first gear and raced for the bedroom to do whatever the Maserati induced in his lower bowel.

In the bedroom, he surveyed some articles of clothing hanging from a table and chair. Three pairs of trousers, three shirts and three pairs of socks. The shoes went with anything, which was irrelevant as they were all he possessed in footwear and wasn't about to change with fashion when there were thousands of miles of wear in them. Grey trousers and pink shirt went fine - resolved in a jiffy. Tell the dog about it later but first the effect of the Maseratis on his bowel demanded attention and with a squeal, he reversed onto the toilet.

People said The Doctor had a lantern jaw, which he liked to shave after a hot shower because his beard was softer and easier to manage. What the fuck did a lantern jaw mean? A lantern did not look like any jaw he knew of and his certainly bore no resemblance. But this was based on memories of lanterns they carried at pantomimes. Perhaps there was a special sort of lantern he'd never come across that looked like a human jaw or at least the sort of human jaw he had.

The Doctor selected a pair of baggy underpants from the pile on the chair and thought seriously of removing the table to improve the bareness of the room. Perhaps he would ask Henry's advice on such an important matter. Nowadays he asked the pilot about important things to check his judgement and see if Henry's treatment was working. Henry told him that putting up curtains would not keep the day away, only the daylight. He'd bowed to this superior knowledge and refused the curtains his maid offered to give him free of charge. After that, he reduced his wardrobe to three of everything requiring the maid to visit seven days a week to do his laundry. This made her feel wanted but also made her tired because she carried the ironing board and iron with her wherever she worked and they were heavy.

'Why does she wash everything in cold water? It take hours Snoops and why doesn't she use the washing machine instead of doing it by hand?' he paused, 'we haven't got a washing machine, that's why, but she could still use hot water,' said The Doctor.

Snoopy didn't answer because she wanted to gather her energy ready for the drive into town on the front seat of the car when The Doctor made casual selections of the pedals with his low profile shoes, raising clouds of dust and occasionally hitting rocks with the side of the car. He only swiped the right side on the way to work because the sea was on the left and he never drove home when he was drunk. Henry often did that and got him into bed with the keys left in the ignition ready for the next morning.

'Snoops old girl, remind me to monitor Henry's driving tonight to see whether the medication I've prescribed is making a difference.' He whistled a tune and pulled on socks of different colours to achieve an unbalanced dress effect, 'God is our refuge and strength,' he said to the dog which made him feel better and added, 'wey-hey,' and danced a jig around the bed until his shoes squealed on the tiles.

Snoopy opened her eyes when the Maseratis began to wear off and watched her master apprehensively. He took some dollar bills from the table, selected a new one and examined it against the morning sunlight to make sure it was genuine. He tore it into small pieces, scattered them about the room but retained a few bits to throw out of the car window on the drive. That made sure the maid couldn't stick the complete note together, which she invariably tried to do. That wasn't the point of the exercise. The point was to tear up dollar bills, not give the woman money.

'Money is boring,' he said and kicked the pieces about, sweating slightly after the jig, 'time to go Snoops.' He opened the French window leading from the bedroom onto the veranda and stepped gingerly into the bright sunshine, eyes fixed on a ramshackle bar at the end of the drive where he liked to start his day with a drink.

When the car started, The Doctor drove flat out in second gear and at the last second threw the steering wheel hard left and pulled on the hand brake, sending the vehicle into a four-wheel slide that brought the right wing crashing into the wall of the bar. He reversed the car away from the wall to point in the direction of town ready for a quick getaway.

'The Earth and all that is in it is the Lord's; let the people rejoice and praise God,' he spoke from the door of the bar.
'I got one ready for you doc,' the barman said and The Doctor groped his way through the chairs and tables to the counter. A single drink and they left for town.

In the car, Snoopy tore off a gentle fart to acknowledge she was awake. It was a technique The Doctor admired and of late had taken to imitating after office hours and which the pilot admitted he envied because he could not make such deliberate sounds of the arse. The Doctor knew this was because of the treatment he was giving Henry. The dog farted loudly but this time in fear as the car went into a slide through the dirt by the roadside when The Doctor pressed the accelerator instead of the brake.
When they recovered the tarmac surface he said, 'penny for your thoughts old girl,' but Snoopy thought nothing while they overtook a slow-moving bus full of schoolchildren on a blind bend that curved sharply

right and which tried to fling the car sideways over the cliff and into the sea. The centrifugal force decreased and she gave a weak thrash of her tail and rolled back from the door onto the seat. 'Keeping quiet this morning old girl. Good thinking,' and threw a hard left, clipping rocks to avoid a taxi.

'Wey-hey,' The Doctor was in high spirits when Road Town came into sight, put his foot down in the main street and skidded into the kerb outside the hospital.

*

2

1964 London - The Embankment

The Chief's pinstriped trousers rode up to show he wore suspenders. He craned forward at the window pulling them higher still above his ankles.

'On my walk from Temple station to the office I pass Cleopatra's Needle, a 3,500 year old obelisk. Erected by the Thames but stolen from the Egyptians ages ago...without receipts of course.' The Ministry of Defence window looked directly onto the Thames embankment, 'cars drive past the needle and no one knows it was shoplifted from the Nile. The Victorians said it was a gift and now time has made it respectable. Whenever Egypt asks us to return it, we become indignant about ownership of our national treasures and demand evidence of wrongdoing. There is no evidence and possession's ten points of international law. The job in hand is like that. Except there are receipts we'd really like to have.'

The Doctor remembered the Chief dressed in pinstriped suits when he was out of army uniform but never guessed he wore suspenders.

He put on his respectful voice, 'knocked for six when you asked to see me Chief. Cold war's been unfriendly for us carthorses.' They were in the offices of military intelligence overlooking the Thames and the Chief of Military Intelligence gave a few seconds of thought before he answered.

'Philby's defection to Moscow last year caused shenanigans in MI6 and rather blighted their good name. Leaves us in military intelligence swamped with offers and grabbing all hands we can...,' he fixed The Doctor with a look, 'even carthorses.'

'Afraid the only pace left in me is slow,' said The Doctor, 'not keen on excitement either. Comfortable walk and a sugar lump.'

'We have a cart that needs an aging dray between the shafts and you could fit. Sleeper job for a couple of years. Up for it old boy?'

'Want to reveal a tad more before I answer?' said The Doctor.

'No can do. Need a yeah or nay. Starts or stops with that.'

The Doctor knew about blind decisions in military intelligence. Turn left or right but only one path led to service heaven.

'Sir, you've been reasonable with me over the years.'

'Return some faith.'

'Give me something extra.'

'Faith doesn't need more.'

'A nod or wink.'

'Best I can do.'

'What's my alternative?'

'The knackers yard old boy. Calling in all the medical favours you've done for your friends over the years won't alter that.'

'So my choice is take the job or retire?' said The Doctor.

'Worse. Personnel chanced to audit your record and tell me you should have been dismissed years ago for your *various idiosyncratic security lapses*...without pension. You need fast rehabilitation, a reinvention of character to prove them wrong. Otherwise, I've no option to get rid on their say-so. You know how people leave military intelligence.'

'Handcuffed by the Official Secrets Act,' said The Doctor.

The Chief craned his neck at the window again and The Doctor saw the suspenders fight a losing battle. The stockings drooped with his own resolve.

'Cleopatra's Needle is engraved with a language thousands of years old. For someone back then, it must have been important to chisel hieroglyphics on Aswan granite as a permanent record of events. What it meant was a mystery until it was deciphered in recent times. History can do that - keep things secret.'

'What makes me the horse for your cart?'

'It's more a tumbrel than a cart.'

'Killing's not my ticket. Hippocratic oath, etcetera.'

One suspender had fallen around his ankle and the Chief spoke to his own reflection in the glass of the window.

'Personal weakness attracts our security men and their archers aim to cull ambivalence. Take you for example. Your file says you radiate weakness and strength in equal measure and that fills our masters with doubt. They ask me which side you'll land on. If the arrow they aim at you should be snapped in half or dipped in poison. Oh definitely, your soldier friends in the House of Commons still love you but they can't stomach the chance of a howler and this one's big. The prospect of being caught turns politicians into cowards so they appoint me as gatekeeper to give them comfort. They want someone to blame. Not hard to spot when a security committee becomes pragmatic and say things like..."final decision's yours Chief," which means, if it goes sour the vinegar dribbles on my head. Don't much like that idea.'

'My record is good.'

Now the other suspender fell and both stockings hung loose, 'a security committee is a bunch of heroes who'll do much to save their own necks. Listen how we save yours. Men like you who fell into intelligence by chance are has-beens. The favours you've done have been repaid and supporters keep you afloat. This is a last shot to baffle the rest. Medicine is good and that religious stuff is virtuoso...keep it going old boy. Turn the job down and I unleash the dogs with no quarter. Yeah or nay old boy. Enough said?'

'Yes,' said The Doctor.

'Well spoken,' he flipped open a cardboard file on his desk, 'here's a twentieth century hieroglyphic to challenge us. Care for a gin while we decipher it?'

The Doctor cared for a gin very much as his Chief knew and smiled when three fingers were poured into each glass topped-up with a thimble of tonic without ice.

'Take us a couple of drinks to get through this lot,' the file was thick, 'share my thoughts while you taste the gin.' He walked to the window and both suspenders were visible below his trousers, 'you've two years to lay a trap. Then, it'll be sprung with honey and you'll like the flavour, I think.'

The Chief said they'd bought intelligence from a rogue agent about a German war criminal hiding epic political secrets. The information was ultra sensitive but others might have bid for it because it mattered more today than World War Two. The Doctor's job was to validate the German, keep him alive and recover what he kept mum about twenty-five years before. Forget revenge; plenty of his Nazi pals strolled round Brazil avoiding the hangman's noose. But, this boy hid exceptional secrets waiting to be unravelled in a pleasant climate.

'Caribbean a suitable place for you doctor?'

'What's the cover for two years?'

'Authentic old boy. Be yourself...medicine...religion...things you like most and we've organised a real job. Stay drunk and we spring the trap when you scream ready.'

'Give me a hint about the endgame?'

'That's too distant to say. For now, live it up. Easy peasy in the tropics with those gallons of gin. Don't kill yourself and don't kill our German when you find him. At least not until we lever his secrets. Relaxed brief for you. Play it by ear for a couple of years and we'll let you know when your infantryman is on the way. Keep a moral distance about the goods we're looking for. Like Cleopatra's Needle, they're stolen but have aged well, and become very attractive in today's marketplace.'

'Easy peasy,' The Doctor said.

*

3

1936 Germany

Gunter eventually found out the exact date he was discovered and remembered sitting outside a large door at the orphanage beside another boy. At that orphanage, children's birthdays were recorded as the day they were found and their age in years was guessed. When he could understand, the nuns told Gunter he was a present from God who was lucky to have different mothers. These nuns usually spoke in German but there were other languages, as the order attracted followers from many countries in Europe. For a time the sisters were concerned that Gunter hardly ever spoke but Sister Maria from Barcelona said they shouldn't worry because she saw in his eyes he was listening. She also observed Gunter was immaculate in his politeness but cold in manner. There was a chill intelligence behind his polite facade and she wondered where God would direct him.

'Father, how do we learn if his remoteness is caused by good or evil?' Maria asked her priest after confession.

The priest replied, 'at his age we discover the prospective man through correction. Cane him until you discover the true nature of his spirit.' Sister Maria shuddered at his advice and never raised the topic again.

Sister Maria was accurate in her observation that Gunter listened. One day when she spoke to him in Spanish, he replied in the same language. Until then he'd spoken in simple German. She spoke a few more sentences to him and was thrilled when he replied in Spanish. He had an absolute pitch memory for words and their meaning. So Gunter became her private language student, as there were no other Spanish nuns in the orphanage.

Maria understood his hunger to learn because there were few toys to distract the children and the nuns were not a replacement for real parents. Sometimes a man came at weekends to entertain the orphans with puppets. He was an old time vaudeville artist that Gunter helped with his equipment and who, in return taught him the skills of his profession.

'You act it for me Gunter. Remember, when your fingers control the puppets they become people to those who watch. In a performance, you need to use different characters. When you switch make your hands still and fix the audience with your eyes like this,' he made his eyes wide, 'don't blink and they will stay with your face…change the puppets on your fingers and take your audience to the new characters. Finger to eyes and back again. Yes that's the way.'

Together, they worked with the wooden puppets he brought for the shows until the pupil surpassed his teacher. He told Gunter their future was in a military world and they began to carve soldiers to use in their shows.

'You have a gift with wood and the qualities of a fine performer Gunter. These are wonderful figures you carve and the toy furniture is beautiful. Perhaps you will be a carpenter. Have you tried making full-sized chairs and tables? But no, for the sisters will take all your time to make things for the orphanage and we lose the puppets. Keep this a secret between me and you.' Gunter loved the feel of his wooden figures dressed as warriors. Side by side, they carved soldiers and when the old man was away, Gunter made miniature furniture props. But he kept his talent secret from the others.

One evening Sister Maria talked to Sister Myja from Poland.

'What a shock when he answered me in Spanish,' Maria said.

'Maybe not. Gunter speaks to me in Polish and I heard him speak English to the child we found abandoned with him,' said Myja.

Sister Maria said Gunter was close friends with Karl. The boys spoke in Polish or English to keep their secrets from German speaking orphans. They discovered that Gunter learned English from another nun.

'He listened to me for years without speaking a word of English,' Sister Mary said, 'but when he started it's like it's his native tongue.'

They realised Gunter had intellectual talents that were valued in a country mesmerised by the nationalism of Adolph Hitler, providing the intellect belonged to a German. And Hitler's brown-shirted disciples were prowling everywhere looking for converts amongst young men. They wouldn't let a religious order stand in the way of their search for Aryan males. Sister Maria and her religious circle took a no-nonsense approach to make sure Gunter and his friend Karl, were recorded as German foundlings. Both were blond and the nuns faked their papers to show them as orphans from German families. The boy's friendship was intense. Each conversed easily with the other in German, Polish and English and Gunter had flawless Spanish. Besides, he possessed a mystifying ability to influence Karl.

A delegation of Hitler Youth officials visited the orphanage searching for teenagers to join their drive for a nation unsullied by the blood of Jews and other tainted races. Gunter and Karl were perceived as textbook Aryans and the nuns watched desolately as they left for *development* training to hate Jews and worship the Fuhrer. The most important official signalled approval when Gunter asked if he could take a wooden military puppet with his few possessions.

After the boys left, the nuns prayed for them. In the following months, they thought about the pair who held hands at the door of the orphanage before separating into military columns at the bark of a Nazi supervisor. They hoped life might be kind to them...but fate would decide.

*

4

The Caribbean - Tortola

Wednesday 20.00 - 16th February 1966

Gunter breathed easily and let the Christmas wind blow over him. He lay on his side and enjoyed the light fingers tracing familiar paths around his spine over the skin down to his buttocks. The delicate hands wandering in a constant pattern over the contours of his back, insistent, again and again but always returning to the same point then starting another circuit he wished would never end. He knew his unseen back better than most people know their own face because pain had etched its image in his mind. Pain could make a man plead for his soul to depart, or if it lessened, beg it to stay. When pain relented, its memory never faded. But there was a special pain that Gunter feared most that lingered from the war. Gunter's dreams were mostly from his past.

Gunter said, 'sleep has thoughts they call dreams. Remember those people we saw dead. You knew they weren't dreaming.' Karl stayed quiet and Gunter went on, 'there's no control in dreams. What you think is what you think. Just lately, I've dreamed about a number. Every dream has this number in it,' but Karl said nothing.

Sometimes Gunter's dreams entered a kingdom where darkness overcame the power of thought. He knew Karl liked him to dream for the passion that followed when he woke yet they never spoke of his dreams. Today he dreamed and didn't resist the sensitive fingers or the Christmas wind blowing through the open window sending him into himself and he slipped away easily.

Conscious now, he turned onto his left side and took Karl swiftly with no warning. Karl was ready and had been the whole time. In a few thrusts, Gunter was finished. This tormented drive for sexual congress almost matched their pleasures of reprieve from death. Tonight they would have sex without the dream and it would take longer but without the extraordinary desire both men had just felt.

>'You slept through to happy hour,' Karl said.
>'Let's go for a drink.'
>'Somewhere different.'
>'There's only one bar here in town,' said Gunter.
>'OK, but could be there's interesting people in it. Maybe the doc is there to gossip. Me and him talked a few days back about a post mortem on some blond guy who drowned at Trellis Bay. He put it down to heart failure although there were a few burn marks on the corpse.'
>'Talk comes easy to a drunk.'

'I guess.'

'Why'd he tell you that story?'

'No reason I know of.'

Karl admired the movement of his lover. Gunter was over forty yet graceful as a cat and looked fifteen years younger. Women liked his arrogance and crawled over him. None of them knew he was gay and thought he played hard to get and so chased more. It was a lost cause. Gunter sank his first beer at breakfast and smoked as if each cigarette would be his last. He stayed thin and never breathed hard when climbing the mountain to shoot. It changed when he turned around. Two men in one skin with a back scarred in regular whorls like a child's potato cutting pressed onto a sheet of paper. Gunter said his back didn't hurt these days.

They'd been lovers since the orphanage and Karl was used to Gunter's unfaithfulness. Gunter's quota of boys increased but Karl believed Gunter loved him more than he loved the others. Karl knew there were many admirers and someday Gunter might cut him out altogether. The rent-boys in San Juan were OK but lately he saw Gunter look hard at other men. Getting old and ditched frightened Karl sick.

'Move it,' Gunter said.

'I like to watch.'

Gunter reached across the bed and squeezed Karl's fingers until they cracked. He relished the flash of pain on his lover's face and felt violence stirring in him.

Gunter said, 'I dreamed of B6174. Do you remember that tattoo number?'

'Not exactly the number, but they only did tattoos at Auschwitz. No other concentration camp except Auschwitz gave the prisoners tattoos,' said Karl.

'Think about the 'B' letter.'

'Men got marked with a 'B' before their number, and women got marked with an 'A' before their number.'

'Think about A6174 and B6174,' said Gunter.

'I remember we trimmed the same number for your blond kid and his mother with the tattoo guys. Only the letter was different,' said Karl.

'May '44 is when that system started with letters and there was only one pair with the same numbers in our unit at Auschwitz meaning there's only one male forearm tattoo for B6174 ever existed.'

'The Polish boy got 'B' marked on his arm,' said Karl, 'all the rest were 'A' women in our unit.'

'And him and his mother survived?'

'That's right. We all got out in the end,' said Karl. 'You got a better memory than me.'

'It was Italia who nudged my memory,' said Gunter, 'the girl who hangs out in the shop trying on dresses.'

'Mixed race beauty?'

'She talks shit and mostly I don't listen but the other day she yaks about who eats in the restaurant where she works and suddenly I do listen,' said Gunter.

'Yeah.'

'There's a guy comes in the restaurant she serves who the pilot brings in with some other passengers off the flight and she notices him because this guy wears a long sleeved shirt. Not usual in this heat. Anyway, after he eats, this guy sits outside to watch the boats. It gets hot in the sun, and she takes him some water. The guy rolls back his sleeves to cool off and she notices a letter and number tattooed on the inside of his left forearm. He asks her to bring him some milk and when she goes in the restaurant, she writes it on a napkin - B6174. She gets his milk, takes another look at his arm, and checks her napkin. She thinks that maybe he belongs to a sect. She doesn't know about the 'B' letter but asks what I think about the number. They do voodoo stuff on her French island and she's scared.'

'What're you saying?' said Karl

'She shows me the napkin and I said it was probably a joke tattoo or something like they do in street gangs. Definitely not voodoo. She says thanks but don't tell the pilot because he goes crazy when she talks about voodoo and I say fine,' said Gunter.

'She tell you how this guy looked?'

'He had white hair. I didn't show interest but she describes the guy like that.'

'The Polish kid and his mother both had white hair,' said Karl.

'I said maybe it was bleached but she was sure it was natural white. She'd never seen hair that white. Then she loses interest when it's not voodoo and plays with the dresses.'

'We don't need this,' said Karl.

'I'll check it out when you go...but after twenty years nobody can recognise us.'

'He was a child,' said Karl.

'Tattooed B6174,' said Gunter.

'We had tattoos,' said Karl.

'They were different tattoos for SS men.'

*

5

The Caribbean - Tortola

Thursday 10.00 - 17th February 1966

Gunter carved the shape he wanted. It was soothing. He fixed on his final creation. He heard a woman's voice in the shop and left his workroom. It belonged to a mixed race girl who was lovely but the wrong sex to interest him.

'Italia,' he said.

Her shy eyes lifted to his face, 'hello.'

'Are you in town alone?'

She giggled and covered her mouth, 'no.'

The pilot's face appeared from a rail of dresses and Henry said, 'you don't seem to have my size,' and disentangled himself from the clothes.

A crazy pilot with a mind as uncontrolled as the air he flew in. Gunter liked him.

'Good timing Henry; I need a favour.'

'Sure,' Henry said.

'Look at this dress,' said Italia.

Henry stroked her hair, 'put it on.'

'Buy me some flowers in San Juan next week and fly them here,' said Gunter.

'Tell me a day before so I get fresh blooms.'

'There's a place near the Borinquen Hotel.'

'I know it,' said Henry, 'what sort of flowers?'

'Suitable for a grave,' said Gunter.

Italia turned a pirouette before the men in the new dress. Her nipples were erect and showed hard through the beige silk. The outfit was gathered at the waist and tied with a blue scarf. The effect was startling and set off her translucent skin. Her slender legs were barely covered by the fabric and she pushed her hips forward.

Henry swallowed hard and Italia checked his reaction. She loved Henry but it was the Frenchman who'd bought her services when she was sixteen. That was a common arrangement for young girls around the islands. But the Frenchman was impotent and used her only to work in the restaurant and when Henry arrived, Italia turned to him for pleasure. He treated the girl kindly in return for her favours, but didn't love her as she loved him. Henry had other women and never tried to hide them from Italia. One day in his shop, Gunter noticed her sadness and guessed why. She cried when he gave her a belt as a distraction from Henry's unfaithfulness.

'Keep the dress,' Henry said, 'take it off when we get home,' he winked at Italia and she reached out to him but he held her away.

'Later,' said Henry.

Gunter chuckled, 'the storeroom is free.'

'No, I have to fly. How much is the dress?'

'A bunch of flowers will pay for it,' said Gunter.

'A dress costs more.'

'But your flowers are worth it to me,' said Gunter, 'it's settled.'

Italia kissed Gunter's cheek. She was the only woman he knew, who didn't repulse him. Italia took Henry's hand and went to the door. For a moment, the couple were silhouetted against the light until they stepped outside. The shop was quiet after the presence of young life. Gunter locked the door and walked to meet Rudolph at the quay where they landed game fish off the charter boats. At this time of day, it was hot and the wind dropped. The oppressive silence was broken by music carried across the water.

Rudolph was working at the quayside to remove the teeth of a dead shark. He was an expert and boiled its jaw until the teeth came out easily with pliers. Rudolph made necklaces for tourists with the teeth. The American who caught the shark lost interest after his picture was taken standing beside it, and gave the fish to Rudolph. He pulled out the final tooth as Gunter arrived.

Gunter bent down, touched the skin of the shark, and ran his fingers down to its tail. Sandpaper over muscle. He admired the pure lines of the creature unlucky enough to swallow a hook. Matched against man in its own element the shark would be the winner.

'Did you get them?' said Gunter and Rudolph pushed over a gunnysack filled with fishing line and spare hooks. Two packages lay underneath the clutter of gear.

Gunter looked around but they were alone on the quay and he took out the smaller package and undid the paper. Inside was a block of resin marbled through with white flashes. Hashish and cocaine mix.

'That looks like the stuff you got last time,' Gunter said, 'buy your kid brother a present,' he peeled off a hundred dollar bill. The second package was bigger and Gunter handled it like fragile china and headed back to the shop.

*

6

The Caribbean - Tortola

Friday 08.30 - 18th February 1966

Gunter leaned on the wooden rail of the patio at the airport bar and Meath gave him a beer. It was eight thirty in the morning. Meath sucked on his cigarette and wanted to talk but Gunter's eyes were fixed on the Piper Apache on the tarmac. There were other aircraft parked and left to rot in the sun. Only the Apache seemed to have the strength to fly away through the scattered clouds over the island. The other dead aircraft were finished and their life in the sky over. A pity to leave them that way, indecent Gunter thought, like not burying the dead.

    Meath said, 'are you flying out?'

    Gunter shook his head, 'no, a friend,' he crushed the empty can, 'another.'

Meath opened the fridge under the bar and bent to pull out the beer, wheezing with the effort. Meath was fragile. Gunter had seen plenty stronger than him give up. Some died of fright before they made it to the gas chambers in the camps. There was something about Meath and his airport bar that bothered Gunter.

'It was sudden at your age to open a bar Meath. What made you do that?'

'Same reason you got a shop and I was bored in the States. This keeps me busy and it's warm.'

'You came here about the same time as the pilot.'

'Yeah,' Meath ducked into the fridge, 'maybe I'll join you. This is on the house,' but Gunter laid a note on the bar.

'You pay after the flight leaves Meath,' he turned away and leaned on the rail.

Voices drifted from the shack where immigration officials fussed over their paperwork. Not much happened at the airport and island bureaucrats made the most of each arrival and departure. There was no hurry because the pilot liked to arrive just before his scheduled departure slot. Henry's flights always left on time.

Ten minutes before departure Gunter looked across to the restaurant where the pilot rented a room from the Frenchman and saw the door open. Henry strolled out eating a bread roll ready to start the morning service around the islands. He reached the immigration shed with the last bite and went inside to file his papers. To Gunter, it seemed like Henry was an old hand on the island but his conversation with Meath reminded him he wasn't.

'Let's go,' Henry said to his passengers and walked across the tarmac to the parked aircraft. Karl trailed behind.

'Leave some beer for me tonight,' Henry shouted to Gunter.

Henry led the passengers to the front hold of the Apache to stow their luggage and a boy carried Karl's bag. Last night was rough and though Karl's face was unmarked, the rest of his body was badly bruised from the cane. The island's remoteness had accelerated what used to be a submission tease with Gunter. Karl found these games getting more and more violent. Maybe it was boredom and drink but Gunter's behaviour didn't hold up. The beatings were like those he gave to Jews in the camps.

Karl walked with tottering steps. He was weak from the caning and never once looked across to the bar. Today Gunter felt sad about things. Not for what he'd done but the sort of sadness you get when someone is going away for a long time. Why was that when it was their birthday next week? Karl chose his own trips with the airline he worked for and held a pass that gave him free travel down to the island. He came once a month so there was no reason to feel sad. Gunter flapped at a mosquito buzzing in his ear to wave off the sadness. There was a new game to play with another man, where sadness had no place.

The passengers climbed onto the wing over the flaps, another step to the door and then inside. Karl let the others go first and it left the front seat empty for him to ride alongside Henry. The pilot liked someone beside him he knew in preference to strangers. Karl strained to pull himself onto the wing and paused after the effort. Gunter waited for him to wave farewell but he turned and slid into his seat and disappeared from view. Gunter felt sad. Karl refused to remember how it was. Things had changed and that's why he refused to wave back. Gunter shivered when the door of the plane closed and the start up ritual began.

First, the left propeller screwed at the morning air and the whine of the starter motor gave way to the splutter of flat pistons and settled to an even pulse. Then the right engine joined in the harmony and snarled at its partner. Now there was life in the machine and it was ready to carry nervous passengers into the sky and climb for the sun. For Henry it was the start of a routine day. As they went past, Karl still looked away but Gunter waved anyway. They taxied onto the runway and he settled against the rail to watch the show. The plane went to the end and turned ready for takeoff. Karl sat out of sight.

Henry checked both magnetos with the engines at high revs. The Apache's nose pointed down the runway at the bar terrace and he exercised the propellers from fine to coarse and fine again ready for takeoff. Gunter recognised the different engine sounds. When full power came on loud, Gunter watched the plane with its retracted undercarriage heading straight at him. Henry missed by a whisker with his wingtip. Gunter stood firm as the monster hurled by ten feet from the ground and turned hard to avoid the building. For a split second, Gunter and Karl locked eyes, and then Karl headed for St. Thomas to catch a New York jet.

'Another beer,' Gunter threw his empty can to Meath, 'the show's over.'

'This one's on the house.'

Karl was quiet on the drive to the airport and said nothing until they stopped at the bridge. He touched Gunter's shoulder.

'Karl said, 'you're too settled here.'

'Settled?'

'You weren't supposed to stay.'

'I have a shop.'

'We never stayed put anywhere then suddenly you fall in love with Caribbean sunshine. It doesn't feel right and now blond B6174 turns up to eat at the Frenchman's restaurant.'

'I'll handle him. There are other attractions to this place,' said Gunter.

'Other attractions don't feel right either.'

Karl's mouth was set hard and he stared at the bridge. Gunter knew he was jealous of his new love interest, The Doctor's nephew.

The plane grew smaller and cold lifted from Gunter's heart. When the Apache disappeared from sight, he still wasn't sure what Karl meant and now it was too late to ask. Meath balanced a lit cigarette on his lower lip.

'I guess none of us would be here if it wasn't for the airport. There's nothing here except the Frenchman's place and this bar,' Meath said.

Meath's voice droned on but Karl's words stayed with him...'things don't feel right.'

'Who's about when the airfield shuts Meath?'

'There's action in the restaurant, when the Frenchman moves his ass.'

'Henry lives at the Frenchman's. You must see him.'

'He takes a beer now and again.'

'How about The Doctor?'

'We see him plenty,' said Meath, 'he likes to drink.'

'He must've been on the island as long as you Meath.'

'I guess.'

'I'll come back later to pick up my stuff from the pilot.'

'Bar stays open,' said Meath, 'most days Henry lands when the sun drops.'

Gunter drained his can, 'keep the beer cold while I dress the ladies in town.'

'Mosquitoes are real bad after dark,' Meath called to him. Gunter raised an arm to show he heard, climbed in his Ford and left in a cloud of dust. Gunter needed the solitude of his dress shop.

*

Best of all, Gunter liked to sit near his shop window where the scarves caught the breeze and whirled in ribbons of flashing colours, caressing his face. Hidden there, he could monitor strangers. Gunter lived with enemies in mind and was vigilant in his Caribbean home. Casual shoppers came in to examine the clothes but once the place was empty, he ambled over to the bar and kept an eye out for trade. It was easy to return if customers arrived. Whenever Gunter needed longer periods of time off, Rudolph looked after the shop if he wasn't working the boats or hustling pool. Rudolph did any work to earn money for his mother and young brother.

A group of American women arrived at the shop and Gunter went to serve them. Perhaps some outsized wraps would fit. They wore Bermuda shorts in checked patterns that accentuated their marbled flesh and he willed them to buy now before they were sunburned and stumbling on elephant legs swelled by sand fly bites after their yacht trip. Today was the time to get dresses.

Gunter said, 'the fabrics are my own design, made in Italy,' and he spun the scarves in whorls of colour to encourage them to buy.

'These are real pretty,' a woman said.

'And unique, no two patterns are the same. You won't find them again, wherever you travel,' Gunter said.

'Are these wraps silk?'

'Pure silk imported from Thailand.'

'My girls at home will love Thai silk bought in the Caribbean,' she said. Conversation was easy because she thought him to be a fellow American.

'Let me know if you need advice,' Gunter acted indifferent.

Gunter stepped outside to let the women indulge their shopping lust. They chose dresses that fitted and some that did not. The women were grateful he allowed them to buy so much and deferred to his subtle arrogance and pale eyes.

'Sir, we didn't leave much behind for you,' one of them said in a southern accent.

'Ladies, your investments enhance genuine beauty,' he escorted the simpering women out and locked the door. Now it was time to relax.

Gunter pushed through rails of hanging garments to a door at the back of his stockroom that opened into a separate workshop. This was a place to enjoy the cleansing effect of manual work and where a carpenter's skill created lasting beauty. The room contained an upright chair and long worktable. There was a rack of tools for shaping wood and a cupboard for drills and lacquers. All that was needed to make fine wooden things. Gunter spoke in German, to his finger puppets hung in a circle on the wall. Wooden heads with cloth bodies, 'seid ihr alle da?'...*are all of you here?* He touched the head of a female puppet, 'but you Gretel, are the only woman in my life and wish me to finish our rocking chair.'

Gunter picked up a hardwood strut and rubbed it with sandpaper. The touch of wood relaxed him. This rocking chair needed months of devotion to equal the simplicity and elegance of those models he made in the war. In the concentration camps, he made chairs using scraps of wood. Time and life were cheap there but his puppets knew this one was made with fine wood.

    Gunter spoke to the puppets, 'all of you will see the chair's beauty and grace. Gretel, you can appreciate the spirit of this part,' he slipped the doll onto his left hand and let her caress the strut. 'We fit it in place and the chair is finished,' he smiled, 'after that my puppet, we move on,' he looked at the other puppets, 'so pleased you all agree.' Gunter connected the pieces of the chair together.

7

1941 Germany

Hjalmar Schacht wanted Hitler to meet his eyes but the Fuhrer went on signing papers and spoke without looking up.

'Pay them; we aren't at war with America.'

Schacht nodded his agreement and said, 'these two American corporations gave us fuel and planes that delivered our victories in Europe,' he was nervous, 'my relationship with them goes back a number of years and they've been crucial in our economic journey to revitalise Germany.' Schacht cleared his throat, 'I guaranteed return of profits from their investments in The Third Reich while I was Minister of the Economy.'

'Schacht's debt of honour,' Hitler looked up, 'but now you have the empty title of Minister without Portfolio,' Schacht couldn't meet Hitler's gaze.

'I don't suggest my current authority is the same, but the Fuhrer will understand the promises of bankers and the deadline for payment is close,' said Schacht.

Hitler held up his hand, 'Herr Schacht, my promise was also given to these corporations and they will be paid.' He searched Schacht's face, 'Churchill crawls to the Americans for help and these payments might help to keep America out of the war. You say the deadline approaches so get it done. The matter is sensitive. Let Himmler oversee the process,' Hitler returned to his papers.

Schacht trembled, 'there is concern that profits were earned using conscripted Jewish labour in our resettlement camps.' Hitler ignored him but Schacht went on, 'and our American partners insist on payment in dollars, gold or diamonds. Right now we have dollars and diamonds,' Schacht's voice was a whisper, 'accumulated from the Jewish confiscation programme.'

Hitler's stare was bleak, 'those are my orders,' he waved him out of the room. It left Schacht to find a soldier with special gifts and nerves of steel to deliver the goods.

*

Gunter called, 'Heil Hitler,' when the officer came in and shot out his arm in a fascist salute. No reply was supplied to a lower rank and the officer circled him. Twin lightening flashes on the officer's collar caught the light but Gunter didn't blink and kept his breathing shallow. Both men wore SS uniforms and the officer held position so their faces were close. One silver and black uniform reflected the other and both wore red

Swastika armbands. Only the badges of rank were different. The officer stayed motionless and said, 'me and you dress the same trooper, but you are special and this mission needs an unusual man. Relax, we have interesting work to discuss.'

'Yes sir.'

'And there's no rank here. We amuse ourselves without military rules. More as friends.'

'I understand,' said Gunter.

The officer opened a pack of cigarettes and withdrew two. He offered a light and Gunter drew hard. He lit his own cigarette and scanned the empty room for invisible listeners.

He said to Gunter, 'for us names are dangerous,' his laugh sounded like a machine gun, 'so we christen you Blanco and me Fritz. From now, until this mission finishes and you come back, no man has higher rank than you – no salutes – no SS shit – you are the top dog Blanco. Think like that and there's enough war left to play soldiers when you get home.'

They were in an underground bunker where a bare ceiling light cast shadows around the walls. Gunter moved about to get a feel for the space but Fritz stayed with him.

'Memorise what we act out in here, with no slips Blanco. If you perform, we both survive so pay attention to your orders.' Gunter listened.

'I have a sore throat; you know what I mean - no Iron Cross.'

'Nor me Fritz.'

'Cure that condition. Win medals for us Blanco.'

When an officer promised a medal, Gunter knew his job was important. But orphans circle the vaguest opportunity to find what else is on offer.

Fritz said, 'on this assignment, you will be a courier with two things to achieve. First, deliver a strongbox and second, bring back some documents. There are four *friends* you will meet to fulfil these two things and we'll talk about them later. There is little risk,' and in a low voice added, 'but if things go wrong you will have a phosphorous grenade that can turn everyone to ashes within ten feet. It is a drastic measure but let us be clear Blanco, should anything appear different from our rehearsal today it will not be right and you must not hesitate to pull the pin. Everyone must burn including you.'

'I understand Fritz.'

He ordered Gunter to sign a document swearing absolute secrecy on penalty of the firing squad. Observing the eyes of Fritz, he guessed death would be welcome from what preceded it if this contract was broken.

'These people you will meet have no real names, just like us, but we must call them something. You are master of the show and I need to tell them what they are called. There are two main actors,' he opened the desk drawer and took out some photographs, 'memorise these faces so you recognise them in the flesh. They are the principals – the two bosses, if you like. Now what names shall we give them?'

'*Die Hexe und der Drachen* are famous German puppets,' said Gunter. 'Witch and Dragon.'

'Then Witch and Dragon are names we use. But Hexe and Drachen will each have a bodyguard who will double as their witnesses during the formalities.' He explained they would meet far away from the war in Europe and the trip was mostly by sea to a remote Caribbean cay.

Fritz took some papers from a drawer and spread them across his desk. They seemed important and were embossed with a Third Reich insignia. There was a knock at the door and the guard showed a man into the chamber. He wore spectacles and his thin lips were puckered into a look of distaste. He was bony and his jacket was too tight. Light reflected from his glasses and he walked to the desk and inspected the papers on it. He signed each one above the name, HJALMAR SCHACHT - eight signatures. He turned away and Fritz accompanied him to the door.

Schacht whispered, 'give him a medal and make sure he is honourably killed after delivery.' Fritz saluted.

When Schacht left, Fritz gathered up the papers and said, 'Blanco, these eight documents are the most important part of our operation.' He pulled a large briefcase from under his desk and placed it by the eight documents. 'You will receive this case from an aide at Santander in Spain before the first part of your journey by sea,' he opened it and showed him a compartment in the lid, 'these documents will be stored here. Make sure you leave four of them at the final destination and bring four of them home to us in Berlin.' Fritz told him about the other signatures that were needed.

He swivelled the case to show the interior. Clamped to the floor of the briefcase was a square metal box with a circular combination lock.

'Here is the strongbox to deliver with those documents. It will be empty when you leave Santander, but at your first port, another aide will insert some valuables in it. For comfort, you will have a phosphorous bomb as a companion for the whole journey at sea.' He rolled a grenade to Gunter and laughed, 'this is a dummy. Your live fire bomb travels with you from Santander.'

Fritz explained the strongbox was thief proof and their mission failed if an attempt to open it was made without the correct combination number because it would freeze.

'And only you could be in a position to play with the numbers - which makes you a dead SS trooper. Keep in mind; just the documents are your business...what goes in the strongbox is not. At Santander, our first aide will check those documents and the combination lock of the empty strongbox works perfectly. At the next stop, our second aide will insert the strongbox contents using the same code and he too will check the documents. These men are the only Germans who know the strongbox combination number and they are senior diplomats,' he hesitated, 'but at the final rendezvous two American men will also know the combination number...and they are *not* senior diplomats.' Over and over they rehearsed every move of the transaction until it was perfect and Fritz said the reception party at the rendezvous would make the same moves. Gunter realised that what went into the strongbox must have great value. Fritz's voice was forceful when he talked through the details of the rendezvous but at the end of the briefing he was quieter.

'When the business is done and you go back to the ship, the captain has a signalling device for you. Outside is a technician to show you how this toy works. Use it and signal your name - *Blanco* - to let us know of your success and after throw the machine overboard.'

'What do I signal if there is not success?'

'Nothing...we are both dead.'

*

8

The Caribbean - Tortola

Friday 19.00 - 18th February 1966

Jayce sat with the others in the failing light of the bar and stared through the gloom at the Ford. There were four of them drinking at Meath's bar and their bags were stacked in a pile ready for collection. Most of it was for the Frenchman's restaurant and Henry delivered those. Today the pilot flew in produce from a San Juan supermarket not available on the island. Because of the aircraft scheduling he positioned a plane from Puerto Rico two or three times a week, ready for the laundry run. So, he brought in groceries for his friends.

With time on his hands, it made sense to load up with food in San Juan and fly it home. Gunter was the first to notice this opportunity when he hitched a ride in an empty aeroplane and made a deal with Henry. The Doctor joined in the scheme though he ate very little and the Frenchman spotted an opportunity for his restaurant and gave the pilot free room and board in return. Henry also inherited the services of Italia who lived with the Frenchman. Henry wouldn't fly stuff for anybody else on the island, even for money. He was odd like that.

Meath lit a charcoal brazier to keep insects away and when it was dark, he turned up a gas lamp that gave a good light to sit in. Meath picked up his beer and sat down between Jayce and The Doctor. Gunter and Henry were in conversation.

Henry said to Gunter, 'your steaks are in the cool box next to the other bags.'

'OK.'

'And I bought a filter for the water pump outside your house,' said Henry.

'It still plays up,' said Gunter.'

'Maybe I can fix it tomorrow,' said Jayce.

'That's great, water pumps aren't my strong point,' said Gunter.

Gunter thought the water pump was a stroke of luck but he needed to measure up Jayce and move in on him. This was new and dangerous territory. Jayce said there were only a few days of his holiday left and Karl was gone. Meath turned up the gas lamp and Gunter shifted to look at Jayce. He was over six feet, about a hundred and sixty pounds and wore shorts and desert boots. Drawing on a cigarette pulled the muscles of his neck into definition. Jayce was whiplash slender and delicate, with a woman's flawless skin drawn tight over high cheekbones that accentuated his eyes. Beneath the mask, Gunter sensed there was madness and he understood how madness happened. Jayce's eyes flickered in the gaslight and stabbed the night with colour. Gunter's urge was stronger than ever...he must possess him.

'Do you like diving?' Henry said to Jayce.

'I'm an amateur.'

'The Frenchman's boat is free to use this weekend. We can dive at Horseshoe Reef on Sunday and pay him for it with the fish we shoot.'

'They say there are wrecks out there...yes I'd like to dive.'

'We'll take an air tank to dive for wrecks if one turns up but free dive to shoot fish,' Henry said.

The Doctor said, 'Henry searches for galleons but returns with fish.'

'One day you'll find a sunken treasure ship,' Gunter said.

'Join us on Sunday,' Henry said to Gunter.

'That's my busy day in the shop and I can't swim.'

'Nobody believes that,' Henry said.

'But it's a good excuse to avoid a dangerous activity,' said The Doctor.

'There's no risk,' Henry said.

'I heard you're a dead shot with a spear gun,' The Doctor said.

'A clean kill doesn't attract sharks,' Henry said extending his trigger finger.

Jayce's eyes flashed in the gaslight, 'are there sharks?'

'Plenty,' Gunter said with his eyes fixed on Henry's extended finger, 'those in the channel under the bridge attack anything.'

'The bridge channel is different,' Henry said, 'Horseshoe Reef has too many fish for sharks to go hungry and look for humans.'

'Let's hope the sharks understand your location theory,' Gunter said.

The Doctor said, 'don't fool with sharks, Jayce.'

'I'll look after him,' Henry said.

Gunter took his steaks out of the cool box ready to leave. There was nothing to gain sitting around with insects. Jayce threw his other bags of food on the passenger seat of the Ford.

'Don't stay late,' Gunter said.

'Not with these mosquitoes,' Jayce said.

'They drive you crazy,' Gunter said and brushed past him to the driver's door. He drove into the night with the car's headlights spearing the absolute blackness.

*

Back in town, Gunter unloaded the car and went for a nightcap. Rudolph sat outside the bar. The usual crowd had gone home and the terrace was empty apart from a man and woman holding hands. He pointed to the brandy and paid for it without speaking. The barman smiled his appreciation at the tip. Gunter swirled the liquor in his glass and looked across the harbour where the moon threw kisses onto the sea and his mood lightened. There were no enemies in sight. He ordered a refill then went outside and sat down beside Rudolph.

'Did you sell any dresses?' Rudolph nodded.

'Go home and give me the money tomorrow.' The boy vanished and Gunter took his drink across the gravel to the shop, fumbling for the keys as he walked. Rudolph would give the money to his mother, not him. That's how it worked to keep the boy sweet.

In the shop, a breeze stirred the dresses to life in the cold moonlight and he closed the door. Near the window were displays of scarves. It was his favourite place to sit. He settled in the middle of them so they cascaded about his head and shoulders and touched his cheeks. Gunter inhaled the silk and moved his head slowly to enjoy the sensation on his skin and hair. With his eyes closed, the scarves formed a protective rainbow around his head keeping him safe.

Gunter forced his eyes open to watch the scarves change intensity in the shifting light and sipped his cognac. This was his oasis where cool silks cascaded in a chill halo around him to ward off danger so he was not afraid. Yet it was just a postponement because things that happened in the war made sure he lived in fear.

Gunter went through the stockroom to his workshop. He used a knife to prise away the lower panel in the tool cupboard and lifted a mahogany chest from the recess. Its corners were protected by wrought silver and there was a plate in the centre engraved 'From KARL'. Karl was thoughtful and generous and this was his finest present.

Gunter returned to his chair amongst the silks, rested the case on his knee, and traced the letters with his finger. Thoughts of going out at first light tomorrow energised him. He locked the shop and went out with the gun case under his arm. The Caribbean silence was broken by the ping of a halyard against a yacht's mast. Intermittently the moon flickered behind clouds pushed across the sky by the trade wind to nowhere in particular. Sailors called this wind the Breath of God. Each time a cloud passed in front of the moon its beauty was obscured but its light decorated the edges of the cloud with a collar of gold. Magic was all about and Gunter relished every second of his existence despite the fear.

Back at home his mind was calm and he needed sleep to rise at four in the morning. He showered then climbed into bed with the gun case beside him and passed into the light doze of a sniper guarding his rifle. Resting for action at first light.

*

9

The Caribbean - Tortola

Saturday 04.00 - 19th February 1966

Gunter woke with the alarm before dawn and smoked a cigarette then dressed in jeans and T-shirt. He took a package from the fridge, put it in his pocket and slipped the gun chest into a bag. It was still dark and he drove fast along the empty road to the east end of the island. Slowly the sun rose to daylight but without heat in it.

To get to Sarah's shack he pulled his car behind a wall near the road and walked up the mountain using the drive to the courtyard of the big house. On the far side of the courtyard, an unmade track led up to the shack. Gunter reached the entrance to the courtyard in front of the elegant building, and paused. He checked but there was no one about and he crossed to the track.

The shack belonged to *Old Sarah* who ran the general store in town. Sarah inherited the shack from her sister who had lived in it on the mountainside. When her husband and son died prematurely, Sarah's sister buried them outside her back door and spent the rest of her days keeping watch over their graves until she died herself. Sarah gave her sister a decent burial in the village cemetery but husband and son remained on the mountain. Since then no local resident would venture up the overgrown track to her shack. It was rumoured the spirits or 'jumpies' of the dead men were unforgiving of trespass and setting foot near their graves risked all sorts of horrors. Gunter rented the shack to go shooting but Sarah believed in dark powers and thought he had a pact with the jumpies. Gunter understood their arrangement was confidential and made generous cash payments to buy Sarah's silence.

For a bet, one drinker with the courage of rum inside him ventured up the mountain to the shack but turned tail and almost killed himself scrambling down again. Fifty yards from the shack, the man heard Satan howl in rage and it took half a bottle of bottle of rum to settle his nerves back in the bar. The other drinkers listened in awe and repeated the story to their friends. People looked away from the shack when they passed because it was not wise to risk Satan's glance.

Satan hissed on the still air and the sound carried to Gunter as he got close to the shack. He gave a low whistle. Stretching from behind the graves a huge cat appeared and rubbed against his leg.

'Hello old friend,' he opened his package and laid out a piece of meat for the cat; a domestic tomcat gone wild that lived on the mountain near the shack. Rats and birds were his favourite food and he liked the raw meat Gunter brought him. The cat spent his days roaming the mountain or in the village at night looking for female company.

Nobody could approach the shack with the cat on guard outside the door. After Gunter left, the cat wandered the mountain but for the time being, he was content to stay quiet until his friend departed. The hut was a fragile wooden box with a splintered door hanging on rusty hinges. Inside was a table and chair and under the table a heater and a can of fuel for cold mornings. The floor was hardened earth and the window just a frame. But the view from the window swept dramatically across the channel spanned by the Queen Elizabeth Bridge and followed the road to the airport. Just over the bridge, Meath's house and veranda sat by the beach. To the north, a backdrop of sea was slashed by Great Camanoe and Scrub Island. To the east, Virgin Gorda had Fallen Jerusalem at its southern tip. On three sides, the mountain was impassable and Gunter felt secure with the cat for company.

Far away, more islands dotted the sea and his gaze wandered from the horizon to the bridge and across the channel. A mangrove swamp reached from the veranda of Meath's house almost to the airport, with a rough trail slashed through it. The airport was closed and nothing moved except waves breaking onto the beach. Gunter opened the gun case where the components lay in their moulded recesses. They formed an intricate collage of metal. It was a nice touch from Karl to have it lined with velvet.

Karl said you could buy anything in New York if you had money but he hadn't been able to get a Waffen SS double claw mount 98k sniping rifle with 'dow' code telescopic sight. There must be one somewhere yet no money in the world could smoke it out. Instead, he got a late model FG 42 with ZF-4 telescopic sight and variant mounting, originally designed as a long-range selective fire weapon for the Luftwaffe but with a capability for sniping. It had never fulfilled the sniping requirement completely but for Gunter it was a joy to handle and deadly enough after years of target practice.

Sometimes, to test his skills, Gunter assembled the gun in the dark, fitting each part by touch. Today there was no such test and he enjoyed the sensation of skin on metal while building his deadly jigsaw. When the assault weapon was complete, Gunter slipped the ZF-4 telescopic sight onto the sight finder of the rifle and locked the swallow tailed mounting plate at the rear with a half round bolt and the holding foot with two toggle clamps. There was no need to remove the cover plates for side and height adjustment to centre the target because he'd adjusted the sight time after time to his chosen target area and could hit a coin at that range. Last of all he snapped in the magazine, screwed on the

'Schalldampfer' or silencer, went to the window, and surveyed the world around the bridge.

Hugged by the first bend on the airport road from the bridge was a freak volcanic boulder, shaped like a miniature pyramid. Local residents claimed it was the monument of a witch. The rock was fifteen feet high, rose to a fine point and its summit was Gunter's target. He rested on the window ledge and snuggled the gun's stock against his cheek. Today his limit was ten shots - five at the monument and five for moving targets. There was plenty of time.

In Russia, he worked alongside snipers who drank Schnapps before they went about their business. Just enough to take the edge off their nerves, but he never needed that help and with the gun at his cheek and eye pressed against the rubber eye guard his metabolism changed down a gear. Heart and breathing slowed. Hand and finger steadied. Calm until the kill. Excitement came when the quarry was hit. In war, it was that special moment when the target stood for a disbelieving moment then sank to the ground reluctantly laying down his life for whatever country. Death captured in fine detail through the sniper's lens. That was the thrill of it.

With a gentle squeeze of the trigger, the first bullet left the gun with a muted 'phut' and Gunter saw splinters fly from the monument pinnacle. Over several minutes, he fired another four shots and after the final one grinned with professional satisfaction. Shooting was a wonderful beginning to his day. Now for a live target to give the cat an easy meal.

Gunter was twenty minutes in the firing position before a bird landed on the near rail of the bridge. He blew its head off and the carcase landed on the single crossway. Patience was a virtue in a sniper. Gunter whistled and the cat lifted its head.

'To the bridge little one,' he called quietly. The cat raced through the scrub, down the mountain and after a few minutes, appeared at the entrance to the bridge. Moving slowly in a predator's crouch he halted a few feet from the dead bird and checked for danger. Through the ZF-4 lens, Gunter saw the cat dart for its prey and head back up the mountain.

Gunter ran out of moving targets with one bullet remaining and thought about leaving. Then, through the telescopic sight, he saw a black fin splitting the water in the channel near the bridge. Hammerhead sharks began loitering there when they built the bridge, attracted to the supporting pontoons. He returned to the firing position locating the fin in the ZF-4 but lost it when the shark went under the bridge. Gunter stayed down hoping it would come through to the other side but after a minute there was nothing and he was about to give up. Suddenly the fin appeared again and he aimed slightly ahead of it and fired. The shark was hit and spun around agitating the surface. Was that blood in the water?

There was another fin behind closing fast and Gunter's pulse quickened. The wounded shark tried to turn but was crashed into a soundless whirligig of lost flesh and blood by its fellow. Shark attacking shark. Gunter's body tingled as the sea turned gaudy red. Blood and nature drew others to the scene and they tore their brother into manageable pieces of oily flesh in no time at all. Just as quickly, the Caribbean settled a shroud of diamond waves over the fragments remaining. Such pleasure today.

Gunter dismantled his gun and made sure every surface was clean and returned to its velvet home in the chest. Today was his first shark kill. He whistled farewell to the cat and scrambled down the track to the courtyard of the imposing house but nothing stirred. Work started late and finished early on the island. There were no curious eyes at this time of day and he sauntered across the courtyard and down the drive to his car.

It was eight o'clock when Gunter went to his shop and put the gun chest away but the smell of cordite was on him to savour. A shower could wait and he started carving. Wood calmed that spirit the gun excited. Grain was warm and metal thrilling and they both had a place. Gunter thought of Jayce and trembled. Think like an orphan and take what you can get. An SS soldier keeps things simple. But Jayce was in his mind and the morning had changed.

*

10

The Caribbean - Tortola

Saturday 12.00 - 19th February 1966

The shower stopped while Gunter had soap in his hair and he cursed the pump, sucking water from his underground tank. He wrapped a towel round his waist, picked up a wooden mallet to belt the pump and went outside. He saw Henry and Jayce crouched over the faulty device.

'You have a water pump that works now; all it needed was a new filter,' Henry said.

'I wasn't expecting you.'

Henry said, 'the price of the filter is a beer.'

Gunter hesitated, 'come in and help yourselves.' He wanted to get inside and wash off the soap but knew they must see the scars on his back and be curious.

The shower worked perfectly and Gunter put his head under the stream to think. His plans for Jayce had gone wrong. He dressed and went to join the others.

Henry said, 'celebrities are waiting for me to pick them up in San Juan. This royal ceremony is attracting them in numbers.'

'Are they aristocrats?' said Gunter.

'Could be anyone who thinks they're important - of course, most of them aren't.'

Jayce said, 'can you drop me off on your way to the airport?'

'Why don't you relax here in town; there's nothing for you at The Doctor's house?' said Henry.

'OK,' said Jayce and Henry left for the airport.

Gunter took Jayce to his shop and they looked at scarves and dresses. Jayce touched them with sensitive hands and was uneasy like a soldier. Gunter showed him the workshop and rocking chair. Jayce asked if he made other things and he said only puppets because delicate woodwork needed time. His company of puppets looked on from the wall. Then Jayce left but they arranged to meet again. There was time for Gunter to prepare for that and things to do now.

*

11

The Caribbean - Tortola

Saturday 17.00 - 19th February 1966

Set back from the road at the end of the hospital drive was a general store and Gunter ducked into the smell of a thousand spices. It was a good smell because the old woman who owned the store kept the place clean and there was no stink of rats.

'Sarah,' he strained his eyes, 'Sarah.' There was no reply but he felt her presence.

'Mister Gunter.'

He smiled, 'where are you?'

'By the grain sacks.'

Gunter followed her voice and weaved through the store.

'Old ladies don't sit on grain sacks.'

'Its peaceful here, my son. And if I don't like them what comes through the door I don't answer,' she patted a sack, 'sit with your Sarah and talk.'

Gunter sat on the bag of grain and gave her an envelope, 'your rent and something extra to buy a new hat.'

'Mister Gunter gives Sarah plenty of money.'

'You can keep secrets old lady.'

'Mister Gunter, have you been on the mountain?'

'Yes.'

'You check my sister's husband and boy?'

'They're lying peaceful in the ground.'

'Mister Gunter, that little thing I asked you a few days past.'

'The flowers for their graves are coming.'

'You a good man to do that for Sarah.'

'They'll be laid by the graves on Wednesday.'

'You make an old woman happy my son, but I'm troubled about you.'

'No need Sarah.'

'In truth, Mister Gunter.'

'Tell me what troubles you?'

'The snake die and that not a good sign for you my son.'

Gunter cursed the old woman and her superstitions. Sarah kept a snake in a bottle and used it to tell the fortune of those who interested her. Only she knew the secret of the snake that never left the bottle and lay waiting to tell her the future of someone she pointed it at.

'Before the snake died he turned away from you and curled in the bottom.'

'You never said you pointed the snake at me.'

'I was checking,' said Sarah.

'Checking what?'

'If you'se a good man the snake will know.'

'You should have told me.'

'I told you now,' said Sarah.

'It doesn't matter,' said Gunter.

'It matters.'

'It's jumpie talk.'

'You go careful Mister Gunter; the snake never died before and it's a warning.'

'Get another snake,' said Gunter.

'I got one,' said Sarah.

'Have you pointed the new one at me?'

'Yes sir and he didn't die.'

'Maybe the old snake was sick,' said Gunter.

'Can't be sure,' said Sarah.

Gunter got up from the sack. The old woman had given him omens before but he felt uneasy about the dead snake.

'Something else my son,' said Sarah.

He leaned close to her wrinkled face, 'go on.'

'When you came through the door it looks like you got fire round your head and it still burning.'

Gunter's mouth went dry and he reached out his hand to the old woman. She rubbed it gently to comfort him. He was cold all over and there was sweat running down his back. He shivered and the old woman felt his hand tremble in hers.

'Quiet my son...maybe my eyes getting old and I imagine the fire. All I say is keep away from trouble and the bad spirits leave you alone. By and by things get better. Be careful. Just be careful.' Karl's words came into Gunter's mind.

Gunter's hand shook when he pulled away from her grip but he was thinking again. It was stupid behaving like the locals and their mumbo jumbo talk of spirits and jumpies. He was the one above all this who rented the shack from Sarah because he wasn't afraid of her graves. It was coincidence she talked about fire round his head. His mind settled.

'I'll be careful,' he said quietly, 'and take beautiful flowers to your graves on Wednesday.'

'Thank you Mister Gunter.'

He left her and edged through the smells to the rays of light, which filtered through the ancient door and pulled it open into the blistering sunlight.

When his eyes adjusted to the brightness, he recognised a taxi driver across the street and went over.

'You OK to deliver that chair to Meath's house in a few days, Gassy?'

'Tell me when to pick it up.'

'Leave it on the veranda for Meath to drive to the airport and ship out. He knows about it. Here's an advance.' Gunter peeled of a twenty-dollar bill and handed it to Gassy.

'My belief is your stuff's safe at Meath's place.'

'You're right Gassy.'

'Let me know when to make the delivery.'

'I'll do that.'

*

12

The Caribbean - Tortola

Saturday 20.00 - 19th February 1966

The Doctor arrived with Jayce. Tonight they served lobster and The Doctor tried to distract his thoughts with food. When that failed, he thought of Henry, but his eyes strayed to Jayce, the infantryman the Chief promised.

They'd chosen Jayce because of his looks, and he wore a woman's personality like an old suit. With a feminine face and slender body, his maleness didn't fit. The Chief picked his soldier astutely to set up the end game and The Doctor thought of their briefing by the Thames two years before. The Chief said, "you've got two years to lay this trap and then, it'll be sprung with special honey – you'll understand." Now he understood the total ruthlessness of his intelligence master because the soldier sent for that honeytrap was his only nephew.

'You seem distant,' Jayce said.

'I was daydreaming.'

'What were you thinking about?'

The Doctor hesitated, 'I was thinking of your mother.'

'Do you think of her often?'

'When I look at you - yes,' said The Doctor.

'They say I'm like her,' said Jayce.

'Yes.'

'I don't remember her well.'

'You have pictures,' said The Doctor.

'I mean how she was - her perfume and touch. That sort of thing,' said Jayce.

The Doctor knew she was a distant mother and never close enough for him to smell her perfume.

'She was beautiful,' said The Doctor.

'Do you remember how she smiled uncle?'

'I'm afraid not.'

'That's a pity.'

'Yes.'

'Do you think she was happy when she died?'

'I think so,' said The Doctor.

'But you don't know.'

'I think she was,' said The Doctor.

'Why do you think that?'

He hesitated, 'the nurse told me she was peaceful that morning.'

'But you couldn't help her – and you a doctor?' said Jayce.

'No.'

'I saw her the night before she died when she was asleep on her bed and she looked peaceful then,' said Jayce.

'Then her nurse was right.'

'Yes uncle.'

Henry was late for dinner and they started without him. Lobster was The Doctor's favourite meal, served in melted butter with fresh limes and hot bread on the side. The barman had reservations about feeding lobster tails to his richest client because the food might sober him up enough to win at pool. Jayce hardly drank and watched The Doctor eat.

'Excellent food,' said The Doctor.

'It'll do you good,' said Jayce.

'So it will,' said The Doctor.

'Is this our cloak-and-dagger adaptation of The Last Supper?'

The Doctor looked across to his nephew, 'not quite, but the chap we follow is a Nazi Judas. Your orders are to stay undetected until we filch his silver and receipts. Meantime lock his emotions for us.'

'My cover is perfect.'

'But we haven't nailed our man or found his pieces of silver...or the priceless receipts.'

'We're getting close,' said Jayce.

Rudolph came through the door and jived across the floor to their table.

Jayce said, 'where's Henry?' Rudolph made the shape of a woman and danced back to the door.

The Doctor groaned, 'one day he'll risk a woman too many.'

'We all take risks. Soldiers most of all,' said Jayce.

'You win fame and glory by defending the monarch,' said The Doctor.

'Shakespeare wrote, "and tell sad stories of the death of Kings: How some have been deposed, some sleeping killed, all murdered." Soldiers make sure the monarch stays alive.'

'Poetic stuff, but you also follow The Queen's orders,' said The Doctor.

'Yes, bought with a royal shilling,' his eyes flamed into blue coals, 'to use me for any task that enhances the realm.'

The other side was resurrected. The Doctor felt his mother's intensity but the flame subsided and Jayce controlled his emotions.

'Doc, I got posters of The Queen,' said the barman.

'We should have one for the house.'

'Take this poster doc,' said the barman.

'They're good for bar trade,' said The Doctor.

'I gonna stick plenty on the walls.'

'Put them up before we play pool.'

'Is they lucky for you?'

'No luck in posters,' Jayce said.

'I gonna put one picture over there,' he pointed at the wall behind the pool table.

'Do it,' The Doctor said.

Henry came in, propped a spear gun against the wall and sat down.

'You look tired,' said The Doctor.

'I am.'

'Take your pills,' said The Doctor.

'I did,' said Henry.

The Doctor reached for his bag and took out a handful of tablets, 'increase your dose to two a day.'

'For how long?'

'Until you feel better,' said The Doctor.

The Doctor handed over the pills with a feeling of satisfaction that he was on the verge of a major discovery and Henry was live evidence. Only Henry's level of sexual activity puzzled him. Perhaps it was a beneficial side effect of the pills, never considered before.

The barman came over to play pool.

'Take a stick doc.'

'Most sporting,' said The Doctor.

Smash – smash – smash. Belting the white on the break and not stopping, until the final ball smacked into the leather pocket. The barman feared

The Doctor when he wasn't quite drunk and became unbeatable at pool. He resigned himself to lose tonight and planned how to recoup their bet by cheating The Doctor's bar account.

'You too good for me.'

'Nonsense, a gentleman plays through his losses,' said The Doctor.

'You'se a great player and I ain't fit for pool with you.'

'Don't flatter me. You don't like losing money,' and he thwacked the white into the packed balls and grunted with satisfaction when a colour dropped in a corner pocket.

'Not so doc,' but grinned when The Doctor hit his next shot so hard the ball flew off the table.

'There's your chance,' and The Doctor stepped away from the pool table.

The spear flew soundless across the table faster than the eye could track and thudded into the poster on the wall. A line connected it to the spear gun in Jayce's hand.

'God,' said Jayce.

'The trigger is sensitive,' Henry said.

'It bust my wall,' said the barman.

'You'll be paid for the damage,' said Jayce.

Henry said, 'that spear would go right through a man.'

'It didn't hit anybody,' said The Doctor gripping the cue with both hands to stop them shaking. A residual shock wave vibrated in the space where he'd stood for his last shot. The Doctor was sick it was Jayce, who'd pulled the trigger and had only avoided the spear with a step away from the table.

*

The Doctor recovered his self-control when they were home and poured a drink. Jayce refused. He stared at the wall and a pulse throbbed in his neck. Jayce and Gunter had stillness in common.

'Remember, you're not working for The Queen when you shoot fish with Henry.'

'I know,' said Jayce.

'Use the spear gun with care.'

'Yes.'

*

13

1941 The Atlantic Ocean

After his meeting with the diplomat in Santander, time dragged heavy in the grey Atlantic. Curiosity triumphed over boredom and Gunter opened the briefcase and checked the document section in the lid. The papers were there as expected and the only item of interest was the phosphorous grenade to use if things went wrong. It was fastened with tape by the side of the strongbox in the main body of the case. Gunter knew what it could do. Burns were not as forgiving as shrapnel. He snapped open the clamps and removed the empty strongbox. The strongbox code had been easy to figure out and Gunter imagined how an orphan would enjoy the treasures it might eventually hold. He dreamed what they could be. His dream evolved into reality with the help of a ship's officer.

The chief engineer was a frequent visitor to his cabin and their relationship developed with great sexual energy. When physical stimulation flagged, the strongbox became a topic of interest. Gunter presented his strongbox conundrum to the engineer and they treated the subject as make-believe. It needed imagination but eventually a solution developed.

As long as they made twelve knots, the captain was indifferent to the activities of his special passenger and engineer. When the artistic side of their friendship grew, Gunter demonstrated his talent at carving wood and made some puppet heads. In return, the engineer showed his metalworking skill. They worked on the strongbox to prepare Gunter's harmless conspiracy with springs and a latch. Both men parted with regret when the ship docked. Relationships at sea were transitory and life went on.

*

In Buenos Aires, the handover by the captain took place on the dock at midnight. The German diplomat who welcomed him to Argentina was nervous. He carried a bag slung over his shoulder, spoke in Spanish and told the captain to leave at once. When the sailor was out of sight, he took the briefcase from Gunter. It needed three edgy attempts to check the papers were in order. The diplomat swallowed hard when his fingers touched the grenade. He spoke Spanish laced with a German accent and his words spilled out in disjointed phrases.

'Go over there where we can't be seen. It's dangerous for me to be on this crazy assignment. If it wasn't direct orders from the top I'd have told them to find another stooge.' They stood in the shadows cast by the arc lights of the docks and Gunter smelled fear on the diplomat. He jumped at every sound and was in a hurry to finish the job and get out of the place. People in a hurry get careless.

The diplomat unclamped the strongbox, lifted it clear of the case and scrabbled at the combination lock. His shaking fingers struggled to arrange the numbered dial in the darkness. Gunter watched him fumble with the numbers until it opened. He shook the contents of his bag on the ground to check them. There were some plain, canvas pouches and a folder. Before he could put them into the strongbox, they heard voices approaching on the dock. Gunter pulled him deeper in the shadows but it was just a few deckhands returning to their ship and they passed by. Gunter held the diplomat tight and felt his body shaking but he pulled free and kneeled to pick up the pouches and folder and stuff them in the strongbox. When he stood up, he panicked, clutched the box to his chest and muttered about the Fuhrer.

Gunter tried to calm him and said, 'close it and you can get out of here.' He pressed the diplomat's trembling hands in his own to settle the man. His shaking subsided and the diplomat nodded that he understood the instruction.

Gunter helped to close the strongbox and both men were sweating when it snapped shut. The diplomat scrambled the combination numbers and Gunter clamped it into the briefcase. It all worked. They stepped out under the arc lights and the diplomat threw his empty bag in the sea. While they waited, he muttered his private mantra to stay calm. After a few minutes, three men hurried down the quay towards them. The diplomat introduced the new sea captain to Gunter and pushed him forward with the briefcase. He scurried off without looking back.

The new captain said in Spanish, 'we leave at dawn and hope our company is enjoyable. You stay with us until my vessel returns to Spain,' he raised his hand to cut short a reply when he thought Gunter was about to speak, 'we know nothing of your plans – just some time at sea together until your rendezvous is achieved and then we can all relax. Follow me to the ship,' the two Falangist guards moved into place behind them.

14

1941 The Caribbean - Bellamy Cay

By the light of the storm lamps, Hexe and Drachen were like their photographs but the bodyguards wore balaclavas. When the boat's engine was turned off, they coasted to the cay and grasping hands hauled Gunter onto land. Immediately the Falangists paddled out into the bay and he was on his own.

'Welcome Blanco,' a bodyguard said in Spanish.

Gunter snapped back, 'let's keep it short...which of you is with Hexe and who with Drachen? We talk in Spanish and you interpret without prompting by me,' the bodyguards stiffened at his tone.

The reception party knew he was there to deliver a prize and was deferential. Gunter took his seat at a plywood table they'd set up. The others stood back and Gunter unlocked the briefcase and took out the documents. First, he called Hexe and his bodyguard over and told the others to keep their distance. Both meetings were to be identical. They sat down opposite him. Gunter told Hexe that when all the documents were signed, those specific to him would be placed in a marked envelope. He produced two envelopes marked HEXE and DRACHEN and told Hexe and his bodyguard to put their initials by HEXE to identify that envelope.

It was all very simple; he showed them another plain envelope to hold his own copies.

'You get one receipt for each product. That makes two documents in total for you Hexe. Drachen gets two papers also. I keep two copies from each of you to put in here,' he tapped the plain envelope. 'My interest is just with these documents. What you and Drachen do with the goods is your business. That freight is in a strongbox inside my briefcase. Here we confirm its delivery to you with receipts, and then you and Drachen may leave. I will clean up after you go, so tonight never happened.'

Gunter's low voice bored into them, 'I say again Hexe, two documents will be yours and two belong to Drachen. That makes four for me. No reason for us to talk unless you notice a mistake, but that's not likely,' he paused, 'now, you both sign these papers. One man's signature is there already and your two are needed to complete things. We do the same paperwork with Drachen,' he gave the bodyguard time to interpret. They signed the documents in a few seconds. 'Hexe, when Drachen and his man have signed, you check the strongbox together. When you agree what stuff belongs to each of you, we can all go home.'

After Hexe and his bodyguard signed, he gathered up their documents while they moved away. Then Gunter told Drachen and his bodyguard to take their place at the table. As they changed places he watched the moonlight play through the branches of the solitary lime tree on the cay. The other pair sat down and completed an identical procedure. Gunter used the same words to brief them. Drachen's bodyguard was slow to sign and struggled to initial the envelope. Then, Gunter instructed them to leave the table and join Hexe and his bodyguard.

Gunter stacked up eight documents on one side of the table and pulled his briefcase close. He opened the lid, took out the strongbox and placed it by the side of the briefcase. He beckoned Hexe and Drachen to the table and handed the strongbox to them. Both principals were anxious to hold it and their bodyguards watched carefully four yards behind them. The figures on their documents needed to match its contents and they knew those figures by heart. Hexe and Drachen were tense and went to tally the diamonds and bonds by the edge of the cay. Both men kept their hands on the box. They knew the combination number to open it and the bodyguards locked eyes on their bosses while they checked its contents. Gunter sat at the table; the night breeze carried their whispers to him.

Hexe and Drachen came back fast with the open strongbox and said the amounts had squared. They handed it to Gunter. He placed the open strongbox next to his briefcase on the table and told them to stand with their bodyguards twelve feet away while he allocated the documents.

'My interest is only with the papers; I will check them and put them in the correct envelopes. Then we close your strongbox and finish this meeting.' Gunter scanned each state paper until he was satisfied. He beckoned the men to the table and placed their marked envelopes on top of the products in the strongbox.

'Confirm these are yours,' a glance and a nod. Gunter closed the strongbox then Hexe and Drachen spun the tumblers.

*

15

1941 The Sting on Bellamy Cay

The puppeteer worked his magic to disappear the bonds and diamonds and substitute them with fakes. Gunter's dummy folder held blank paper and his canvas pouches were filled with ball bearings. These replicas rested on a false strongbox base supported on springs and hidden in the briefcase. The base waited for transfer onto the genuine floor of the strongbox using small finger grips to make the switch.

Gunter's sea voyage gave him time to practise moving the fake base with his left hand while holding documents at eye level in his other. There was plenty of space in the briefcase to accommodate the genuine items thieved from the strongbox. A plain envelope was hidden flat inside the briefcase wall, and he palmed it out of sight behind the briefcase ready for the switch. On view to Hexe and Drachen were their marked envelopes and a single plain one to receive Germany's four receipts. The reception party expected to see those. They would not expect a phosphorous grenade and would not see that.

When Hexe and Drachen returned the open strongbox he placed it tight against the side of the briefcase, leaving both lids vertically open and told the principals to stand with their bodyguards. They moved away as instructed while Gunter carried out the document inspection. They could see his upper body above the raised lids of the briefcase and strongbox. The vaudeville artist's hymn went, *"help the audience see what they want...then do what you want"*. Gunter knew how to keep their eyes focussed on the documents elevated in his right hand that he checked and inserted into three different envelopes with plain sides facing them. They would not guess that their genuine receipts went into his personal envelope palmed from the briefcase. Nor would they guess what he did with his left hand below the level of the lids between insertions. But then why would they suspect anything at all because the transaction had been scripted in fine detail for them by Fritz?

Eight documents were lifted up for scrutiny. Gunter stooped forward and kept his eyes just above the level of each one. He considered every paper deliberately for a minute before giving his nod of approval. There was no hurry and the reception party locked into his eyes and relaxed. During the scrutiny of the first three papers, his left hand transferred the genuine contents from the strongbox and dropped them in his briefcase – right to left. During the next three he transferred the false strongbox floor with its fake contents and phosphorous grenade onto the genuine floor of the strongbox – left to right. The grenade was invisible in its own canvas pouch and he clipped the firing pin into the latch before the last document was raised to eye level. The release of the springs under the false floor would do the rest when the lid was unlocked.

Gunter had stuffed the marked *Hexe* and *Drachen* envelopes with blank notepaper while the principals counted their booty. The envelope palmed from his briefcase now contained their state documents. Inside the strongbox, the bearer bond folder held blank paper and the canvas pouches contained ball bearings. None of that mattered when the strongbox was closed and greed beat suspicion.

Gunter nodded he was done, 'please come over and check,' and palmed the envelope containing their genuine receipts into his briefcase. As they approached the table he lifted the plain envelope they knew held Germany's receipts, dropped it in the briefcase and closed the lid to show them his part of the business was over. Hexe and Drachen came to Gunter's side of the table and nodded acceptance of the named envelopes he'd laid face up on top of the dummy goods in the strongbox.

'Our business is finished,' Gunter drew on the strength of rehearsal to force the lid closed against the springs under the false floor. German engineering won through and it snapped shut and primed the phosphorous grenade. With frantic hands, Hexe and Drachen spun the dial to lock the strongbox and secure their goods. 'This becomes your property when you reach international waters. Under no circumstances, open it before. That was agreed by our superiors.'

But, their minds were gone from the cay and Hexe and Drachen wanted to get away. Gunter was of no further interest and they left for their yacht escorted by the Falangist guards. In deep water, opening the strongbox would prove unforgettable when the phosphorous charge exploded like a small sun triggered by release of the grenade's firing pin. Everyone within 10 feet vaporised as if the reception party had never existed; just as Gunter, the courier, didn't officially exist in this corporate transaction. As to the contents of the strongbox, plain paper and ball bearings were cheap.

When he was alone on the cay, Gunter sorted out his plunder. Folded tight in a corner of his briefcase was an oiled, silk bag and he opened it to stow the treasure. First in went the diamonds, second, the bearer bonds and last Hexe and Drachen's genuine receipts. He closed the silk neck of the bag with a drawstring then used a metal collar and key to seal it. His ship's engineer said these bags were made for Chinese smugglers to carry drugs and stayed waterproof for fifty years when the collar was on. Gunter had less time in mind.

He kicked the table and chairs into pieces, used a board to scrape away the soil at the roots of the lime tree, squeezed the bag between the wooden arteries, and forced it upwards towards the main trunk. It was invisible in the womb of the tree after he packed the soil tight and stamped it down to protect the base from Caribbean weather.

'Congratulations Fritz, your direction was perfect in everything that matters for Germany. In my briefcase are four receipts to show our transaction was a success. They will cure your sore throat and give you an Iron Cross. The other four receipts are safe too. I will look after them personally, along with those diamonds and bonds. They go to a better home than you thought but only Gunter knows where they rest. Heil Hitler.'

Gunter watched the reception party cross the bay and thought about his ship's engineer with lust and a gift for working metal who solved the strongbox conundrum. The engineer said the job was simple. Gunter insisted on springs for the false strongbox base when he saw how to arm the phosphorous grenade and asked the engineer to weld a small latch on the inside wall of the strongbox.

Plain canvas pouches and a folder were items easily found during his journey through the Atlantic. Diplomats in Spain and Argentina believed Himmler's personal agent enjoyed total integrity. Gunter could do no wrong for them because their preoccupation was sidestepping danger. The choice of diplomats with jellied nerves solved the problem of the strongbox code for him.

'Happy birthday my Fuhrer,' the diplomat in Santander sang under his breath to calm himself. The 20th of April 1889. No soldier forgot the Fuhrer's birthday and the strongbox code was cracked as 20041889. The second diplomat panicked worse and left the combination number visible to Gunter on the quayside in Buenos Aires. By then, Gunter could have opened the strongbox for him. More sense for Gunter to risk his life for bonds and diamonds. Dying for the SS got a medal but the strongbox was worth living for and justified a firework display on the yacht.

*

Gunter reminded Hexe and Drachen the strongbox must not be opened until they were in international waters. There was nothing further to delay them and he signalled his guards to escort them to their yacht. The reception party was exhilarated and hustled into their dinghy and pushed off with the Falangists alongside. Their boat crabbed over the moonlit bay with the strongbox resting between Hexe and Drachen. The bodyguards watched Gunter's silhouette against the storm lamps on the cay.

Gunter left his briefcase with the Fuhrer's receipts at the edge of the water and a lamp burning next to it. After that, he threw the wooden debris in the sea and waited for the Falangists to return. He stepped into the launch with his briefcase and dropped the lamp overboard. There was enough moonlight to guide them past the yacht with the four man reception party huddled in the stern. They didn't wave and the Falangists headed for the freighter. Onboard, the captain gave him his signalling toy and Gunter sent a coded transmission from the wireless shack. Afterwards he dropped the machine in the sea and scanned the night until he saw fire on the horizon. Darkness settled back and he fell asleep. When morning broke, everything was perfect. The signal he'd sent was *Blanco*.

*

16

1941 Washington DC - FBI Headquarters

'Me and you understand each other where others couldn't get near Martha,' he said in a voice used to being listened to, 'maybe I stuck out to hire a woman agent is why,' he raised his hands as a question to her, 'maybe that's what brought us together first off Martha?' but she cut him short.

'Since when did you chase *maybees*...you want *for sures*? Agency folklore - get the evidence and find out <u>for sure</u>. That's why I'm here – to find out for sure why I get passed over for promotion when evidence in my records says I should be moving up. It's not right from where I sit.

'Yeah, let's keep it right Martha. I can do that but you got a problem with your mouth. Open it in the office and people listen as if you were a priest. When you get fired there's no listeners. And you know what, after you get fired people shit when you tell them things about the FBI. Then nobody wants to hear.'

'You plan on firing me?'

'Worse things happen.'

'Not to me.'

'Step away from the promotion you came to talk about and think survival, Martha.'

'Now you're my saviour?'

'I'm your boss,' and suddenly the voice that was used to being listened to had ice vapour streaming off the words.

'No kidding,' said Martha.

'Think about it. You got the director of the information business of the USA in front of your eyes and you think you can rock his ass. No Martha,' his voice got colder, 'listen-up.'

'I'm listening.'

'You got noticed in the bureau,' he opened a drawer and took out a file, 'you never saw this but it's got MARTHA GOLD typed on and you don't know what's in there.'

'My personal file. I got access rights.'

'Wrong Martha...it's my personal file on you and you got no access rights. Now let me show you how threats work best when you have information.'

Martha sat on a hard chair with a wide desk between her and the boss. He was small and when he stood, to walk round the desk, didn't seem to grow any taller. There was no other furniture in the room except a mirror and a large safe and as he walked past it, he tapped its door affectionately and stood behind her.

'In there is information on everybody who is anybody in the USA. There's a guy watches through that mirror if I get visitors, Martha. We got a signal you'd never guess, that says I'm in trouble and this guy shoots whoever's there except me,' he chortled, 'kind of defeat the purpose if he did. But he's necessary. You'd be surprised the affect information in that safe has on folks that come here. Worst of all they don't know if it's real. Like you don't know what's in that folder. You make a move for it, you get shot.'

'Not a chance,' said Martha.

He said, 'see how information demands attention. *Maybe* it's real and *maybe* not,' now he laughed, 'what folks imagine about information on them is that <u>for sure</u> somebody will believe it. Bravery goes out the window faced with personal information. You gone weak Martha?'

'No.'

'You should. There's *maybe* enough in that file to send you to the chair or get life <u>for sure</u>. You fucking Jewish bitch come in shouting about promotion, after what I did for you,' he calmed down and went behind the desk, 'you've been freelancing for years since you were hired by the FBI. Hired by me in person. It's all in there.'

'Fuck you.'

'Old stuff would get you time - *maybe* life but it could turn things hot electric-chair-wise if the USA is at war.'

'And maybe you're bluffing,' said Martha.

'*Maybe...for sure* - you're the expert.'

'What's the deal?'

'That I own you. In that file is phone tap evidence of an arranged meeting tomorrow with your sponsors in New York.'

'And?'

'I want the lowdown after that meeting on what they think you can do for them.'

'I got a choice?' said Martha.

'Tell me about the boys in New York and your file goes in the safe. Keep quiet and it goes to internal security. The choice you got is stay with me and I cover your ass. What you get from your boys is handed to me in person. I got files on them ready and waiting for your intelligence. On the upside, with me as partner you get the juice on them when things develop. These guys and their associates are yours in FBI territory. It's a great deal.'

'OK, it's a deal,' said Martha.

'Under pressure you think fast. Now, if your guys are so smart why'd they need you...my turn to listen Martha?'

'They're flat stumped,' said Martha, 'that means they told me too much. A big payment to their corporations went missing.'

'Give me detail.'

'What I know is that German brass promised to compensate these two outfits for their investment in German industry. When these American corporations shout time to pay and ask for their dough, a drop is organised in the Caribbean where the arrangement is easy to deny.'

'Why not do it clean and legal?'

'Because of the way German money was got to pay them.'

'What sort of way?'

'Exit money to let Jews out of Europe. Money from Jewish slave labour...that kind of money. These corporate gods had to level that detail to hire my services because I'm a Jew. Other features are vague.'

'Mmm.'

'The swag went missing along with the boys that snapped it up. These corporate Gods tell Martha there's dirty work happened and find the dirt.'

'Make them believe you got extra up your sleeve...a little something you can lever from your government contacts. See what that brings.'

'You bet,' said Martha, 'my opinion from their call is they're on edge.'

'I heard that on the tape.'

*

17

1941 New York - Algonquin Hotel

When there was no contact from the yacht for two days, they rang her. After it was missing for four days, a meeting was scheduled with Martha Gold. To discuss things face to face they arranged to meet in a suite in the Algonquin Hotel because New York suited both men and Martha could travel. They arrived by limousine, with armed guards to hurry them through the bar to the rickety elevators and were left alone with coffee and water in a faded suite. Powerful men like to be flanked by subordinates but today they were alone.

Martha Gold came in with a dossier and closed the door. Both men knew the woman was employed by the FBI. Her work for them was freelance and undeclared to her employer. It was lucrative and illegal. Martha sat down and took out her papers. One man was thin and wore a black suit. The other wore grey and a hat.

'Seems you boys got a mystery, that doesn't hold water any which way it's viewed except one. The commercial transaction was done. That's my understanding.'

'You understand right,' said the man in black.

'Sir, correct me if I'm wrong,' said Martha, 'but the party delivering payment was from Spain?'

'A Spanish courier,' said the man in the hat, 'part of a fascist network that made for safe politics.'

'Kind of sensitive, I can see. Does your German principal claim the goods were handed over?' said Martha.

'He knows they were handed over and we don't want to unsettle that goodwill with questions. It's not his business if we didn't get the funds. Why you got hired is to sniff out the dough,' said the man in black.

Martha settled back in her chair and reviewed the mission again. Two agents and two bodyguards sailed on a yacht via a planned route to a Caribbean cay for a business transaction with a Spanish courier. Track and timings en route were verified by radio and the weather was fine. The yacht's seaworthiness was confirmed on arrival at the rendezvous, as was the sighting of the freighter carrying the Spanish courier. The yacht left on time and its radio signal confirming a successful transaction was received and acknowledged. There was no reason to question the weather and the integrity of the agents and bodyguards was guaranteed.

'Tell me where the fuck they are?' said the man in the hat.

'We can find them if they ran,' said the man in black.

Martha said, 'they've gone...my doubt is whether they wanted to go.'

Six days had passed since the first radio signal without any contact. There was merchant shipping in the area but no reports of a sighting. The Puerto Rico Trench was deep water and conceivably the boat had sunk. It was also possible the crew had elected to sail to another destination.

'Not possible,' said the man in the hat, 'these were bought men. We owned them between us.'

'We set it up so one pair didn't trust the other. They'd eyeball every move the other made,' said the man in black.

'Gentlemen, I need the facts to cover all the angles, said Martha, 'you never said what the nature of the goods were, that were delivered and went missing,' she saw them exchange a look. There was a pause.

'Dollar bearer bonds worth ten million bucks,' said the man in black.

'And?'

The man in the hat said, 'cut diamonds worth many times that,' both men squirmed.

'Tempting amounts for a major thief but my guess is too hot for amateur hoods to fence. That sort of money must've gone somewhere or been sunk. Let me do some research with the navy.'

'What kind of research?' said the man in black.

'That, sir, is classified information and will remain so for national security purposes.' Martha picked up her dossier and walked to the door. She turned with her fingers on the handle, 'our secrets keep us three in spitting distance. But let me warn you that receiving payment in dollar bonds and diamonds stolen from European Jews would finish you both if it became public,' she opened the door and left.

The man in the hat said, 'she knows how to keep us close.'

The other man was bitter, 'why'd you pick that cay for the drop?'

'I grew up round there. Nobody knew about a British dot in the Caribbean and the courier was Spanish. You agreed it was *the* place for a phantom transaction with no American connection to Germany or Jewish labour. The cover was fireproof,' said the man in the hat.

'So fireproof we can't trace anything. That's a great result from a phantom transaction,' said the man in black, 'let's get out of here.'

18

The Caribbean - Tortola

Sunday 08.00 - 20th February 1966

Sunday was The Doctor's favourite day of the week but today the weather was oppressive and the Maseratis didn't shift his sense of foreboding. Snoopy left most of her fish breakfast. The Doctor heard Henry's car arrive much earlier to pick up Jayce but stayed out of sight until they left, then squealed about the corridors on his tyre shoes searching for his unease. There was no answer in the house. He prepared two state prayers for his sermon. The Doctor preached at a local church. He finalised his text ready for the evening service.

*

That night the congregation filed in until the church was full. They were good people with a simple attitude to religion and The Doctor was careful not to confuse them with too much dogma. Innocent faces looked across the table that served as an altar and he delivered his summary of God's laws.

'Thou shalt love the Lord thy God with all thy heart and with all thy soul and with all thy strength. And thou shalt love thy neighbour as thyself.' Some of the congregation praised the Lord and he waited for quiet, 'this is a commandment and has been written.' He leaned forward on the altar and the silence was heavy as they waited for the next words.

'Thou shalt love thy neighbour as thyself,' many knew what he was about to tell them because he often preached the message, 'think what those words mean. Consider how they link with other commandments.' The door at the back of the church opened and Italia slipped in pulling Henry behind her. She was God-fearing but Henry was not.

'Thou shalt not murder. Obviously, if you love your neighbour you won't murder them,' the congregation nodded agreement and a few murmured their endorsement of God's words.

The shutters of the church windows were open to let in the cool of the evening but there was no breeze and The Doctor heard a car door close in the still air.

'Another commandment says that thou shalt not commit adultery,' he held his arms outstretched for their response. They chanted, 'Lord, have mercy upon us and incline our hearts to keep this law.' The Doctor went on, 'this can be confusing. God tells us we must love our neighbour but not our neighbour's wife or husband so much that we are tempted to commit adultery.'

There was an uneasy shuffling of feet around the church and Henry flashed a smile.

'Decide what God means by love. Does he mean the physical love between a man and a woman who marry or the sort of love a mother has for her children or a spiritual love only he understands? There's no easy answer. You know what God means by love when you look into your heart for his meaning and strip away self-deception. On judgement day, when your soul reaches the Kingdom of Heaven where there is only truth, you cannot repent. Loving your neighbour is no excuse for committing adultery.'

A girl wiped away her tears. Most of the island committed adultery and The Doctor warned them about it on Sundays. It was different on Monday. God's laws faded on weekdays and the congregation settled down. They knew The Doctor would comfort them with a story after his warning.

'You might have heard of Doctor Faustus. Not a Doctor of medicine like me but a learned man who knew so much of philosophy and culture they called him a Doctor. He lived a long time ago in Germany in a town called Wittenberg and possessed everything that knowledge could give - except wisdom. He was not a wise man and wished for impossible, worldly things. And do you know how he got them?'

'No,' they answered.

'He sold his soul to the Devil,' said The Doctor.

'Lord have mercy.'

'He made a pact with Satan,' he paused, 'Faustus promised his soul to the Devil if he gave him everything on earth he wanted, for twenty-four years. Satan didn't take his soul right then but after twenty-four years he returned to settle their bargain. Twenty-four years is a long time. Nearly forever to enjoy anything you want.'

The Doctor gave them time to think about this and searched for Henry's eyes but he stared out of the window. Italia looked at The Doctor and her loveliness astounded him. Yet the pilot went with other women.

'All good things come to an end and just before his twenty-four years were up Faustus made a last request to Satan for a woman called Helen of Troy who was supposed to be the most beautiful women who'd ever lived. Satan produced her from history as a vision but without substance. "Sweet Helen make me immortal with a kiss," Faustus said, "See she sucks forth my soul," but it was not the vision of Helen who'd come for his soul - it was Satan. He told Faustus to leave with him for hell but the Angel of the Lord appeared and told Faustus to pray for redemption so God might forgive him and take him to heaven. Satan told Faustus if he prayed for redemption that he'd be tortured worse than any man alive. Even at the end, Faustus chose to believe Satan and went to hell to suffer for eternity when he could have repented and entered the Kingdom of Heaven. God says that it is never too late to repent and receive his forgiveness.'

The Doctor saw a white face at the window but it might have been moonlight.

'Doctor Faustus was clever but not wise. When you leave here be wise and repent your sins. Ask God to forgive you and he will.'
There was a chorus of hallelujahs from the congregation and they set themselves for the escape clause The Doctor offered every other Sunday.

'If you are tempted by Satan to love your neighbour too much and commit adultery, God will forgive you if you repent. He can forgive all sins if in your heart you are truly sorry. Whether it's the end of a day or the end of a lifetime it's never too late to repent. Offer your soul to God and the Kingdom of Heaven will be yours.' The congregation unanimously repented in preparation for the week ahead.

The Doctor stepped back from the makeshift altar to show the sermon was finished and the congregation eased themselves in the hard pews. He stuck a picture of The Queen on the wall.

'As you know tonight there is a special service. First, because our Queen will visit next week and we have a prayer for her. Second, because after the service there is *a meet* arranged to raise money for a new church piano. Let us pray.' The congregation bowed their heads.

'Almighty God, the fountain of all goodness, bless our Sovereign Lady, Queen Elizabeth, and all who are in authority under her; that they may order all things in wisdom and equity, righteousness and peace, to the honour of your name, and the good of your Church and people; through Jesus Christ our Lord. Amen.'

While he recited to bowed heads, there was a second flash of white at the window. Another moonbeam. Henry stared into the night and The Doctor prayed his messages were heard by him. But, Henry didn't care because Satan controlled his soul.

'That ends the service and we move on to the meet. Let's have the musicians over there and the rest of you form a circle. You know how.' The Doctor put a bucket on the altar.

A *meet* happened after a service when the congregation danced a conga round the church in time to the rhythm of a band. Whoever was in front of the bucket on the altar when the music stopped threw in money. People brought small coins to keep the fun going as long as possible and a good meet lasted for hours.

The guitarists took up a beat and the conga circle moved with their natural Caribbean rhythm. The Doctor stopped and started the music. Henry limped behind Italia and fell into time with her rhythm and the beat of the guitars. It stopped when Henry passed the bucket.

Henry whispered to Italia, 'what do I do?'

'Throw money in the bucket.'

'I've no coins.'

'Put in paper money.'

There was a cheer for his five-dollar donation. Then the band played on and they danced until Henry limped past the bucket again and it stopped.

The Doctor leaned across the altar and said in a low voice, 'money's boring dear boy. Throw in your filthy lucre.'

Henry threw in another five and said, 'that's enough,' the dancers moved him on.

The rhythm was strong, the beat of the dancing feet was infectious, and The Doctor moved behind the altar jigging back and forth...turning and spinning. He rested to catch his breath and stopped the music when Italia passed. She dropped in a coin and returned his smile but her cheeks were wet and the tears that ran down were not those of happiness. The man with his hands about her waist was a stranger. Henry had gone leaving his lover weeping in a church.

*

Italia left the church with The Doctor and went to the bar.

'Will you join me?'

'I don't drink alcohol,' said Italia.

'Perhaps some lemonade while we talk.'

She wept and he put his hand on her arm.

'An hour with me is better than sitting alone in the Frenchman's restaurant.'

'Yes, it's quiet there on a Sunday,' Italia said.

The bar was empty and the squeal of rubber on the floor roused the barman from his doze.

'Doc.'

'Sorry to disturb you old boy. My dear what would you like?' The shake in his voice betrayed his emotions.

'Lemonade.'

'And my usual poison,' said The Doctor.

'Right away.'

The Doctor put a coin in the jukebox, turned down the volume and went to join Italia. Her skin was golden and he thought her perfect. It was time to make amends for his life as a doctor in military intelligence.

'Your tests show you are pregnant.'

'I see.'

'What will you do?'

'Whatever Henry wants.'

'The baby is yours,' said The Doctor.

'I don't care. Just what he wants...get rid of it.'

Tormented hands betrayed The Doctor's agony but he forced them together to plead with her.

'My dear,' he choked, 'you must not have the child killed while it is still in you. That is against God's law and the law of nature.'

'God understands what Henry wishes. I love him more than life. More than God if you have to know,' said Italia.

Her anguish was too much for him, 'what if I can persuade him to let you have the child.'

'He will not allow me to have a baby.'

'But if he says yes, will you have it?'

'If he tells me so, but he's a restless man and with a child would leave. Promise to return home and be gone one day. You saw tonight. There are always other women.'

'If I told him I'd make the child my own and keep it, he'd listen,' said The Doctor.

She stared at the table, 'why would you do that for another man's baby?'

'A special baby.'

'But still, why would you do it?'

'Life is precious.'

'Not precious where I was born. On my island, life is cheap. The Frenchman bought me as you could have bought any girl from a mother without a husband. Do I sell my baby even before it's born?'

'For me your child means redemption. Like Faustus I'm corrupted and your child is a way to achieve salvation.'

'You would make a wonderful father,' her eyes glistened, 'but say nothing and perhaps Henry will stay longer - even a single hour as your Doctor Faustus did with Helen. For an hour with Henry I would hand my soul to the Devil,' said Italia, 'after that hour I will ask him.'

*

When Henry came into the bar, The Doctor thought Faustus was lucky compared to Italia's hell. Henry limped across the room with a middle-aged white woman. He pulled up a chair and sat down with a sigh of relief.

'Stood on a sea urchin doc.'

'Fall in at 09.00 tomorrow at the hospital. Whip the spines out in a jiffy,' said The Doctor.

'Definitely,' said Henry.

'Local jab and in ten minutes you'll be good as new.'

'Let me introduce you to a visitor from the big house that overlooks the bridge,' Henry said.

'Pleased to meet you,' The Doctor touched the woman's fingers.

'And this is Italia who works in the restaurant where I live,' Henry said to the white woman, 'she's from a French island.'

Italia murmured, 'I will go.'

'My pleasure to drive you home,' said The Doctor.

Henry said, 'no, I'll drive Italia and you take my guest to her house on the side of the mountain. The stars will guide you up the drive.'

'Of course,' The Doctor said.

'Your place has a wonderful view of the bridge,' Henry said to the white woman.

She answered, 'make sure you join my get-together on Wednesday morning and watch the opening ceremony from our courtyard. You may never get that close to The Queen again.'

'Wouldn't miss it,' said Henry.

'Come back here after you drop Italia,' The Doctor said.

'Is it important?'

'Things to talk about.'

Henry said, 'think about how I dodge the trap that claimed Dr Faustus and we can talk about that,' and went out with Italia.

*

19

The Caribbean - Tortola

Monday 09.00 - 21st February 1966

Before morning surgery, The Doctor thought about Henry and his struggle with women. Henry owned a magnetic personality and there was no doubt about Italia's love for him. But Henry was unable to return it. Then, for no reason, Gunter and Jayce inched into his mind, but they were different. Something about them slipped away when he tried to nail his thoughts down. Perhaps Henry understood.

Henry's face was warm without smiling a lot. He was generous and women worshipped him. Giving was natural but he was irresponsible and shattered the women he touched. It was dangerous to stare into his brown eyes and look for anything less than a broken heart. Henry was transitory. A passing cloud who wanted love by the hour yet women found him irresistible. Some forgave him and some hated him when he left, though no malice was intended. They all wanted more than Henry offered and were mystified when permanence was not an option. Italia understood that. Henry was an enigma to a doctor in military intelligence and The Doctor wanted to solve the puzzle.

*

A black Nurse laid sterile paper on the bed.

'Thanks,' Henry said and patted her backside before stretching out.

'I didn't see you for a while Henry,' the nurse said and ran her fingers down his bare legs.

'Right now I need sympathy because my foot hurts, so please stick around.'

The Doctor called from the next room that he was ready and the nurse moved away from the bed.

'Stay with me, I don't feel great.'

'I'm staying,' she said and took his hand, 'focus your mind on something special to relax.'

Henry fiddled with the sheathed knife round his neck and drifted away to yesterday's dive on the reef with Jayce.

*

They loaded the boat to go diving as the sun came up. There was a cool breeze.

'This is nice,' said Henry.

'Good weather for Her Majesty's visit,' said Jayce.

Henry carried an air tank along the jetty and stowed it in the powerboat.

'The other night I told you the air tank is only used for wrecks,' said Henry, 'otherwise we free dive at a great spot I know.'

'Where's that?'

'A place on the reef called White Horse. It's a coral heap that sticks out of the sea and attracts the kind of fish the Frenchman likes to cook.'

They headed west to clear the southern tip of the reef, turned north and anchored by the coral outcrop.

'There are shipwrecks sunk out here, but I never find them,' said Henry.

'We might get lucky today.'

'Let's shoot fish for the Frenchman. He loves to serve grouper to his customers.'

Their silence was broken by a crash of thunder.

'What was that?'

Henry said, 'dynamite.'

'Who uses dynamite in the sea?' said Jayce.

'Rudolph - he dynamites along the reef and hauls in fish that float to the surface,' said Henry.

'How does he get dynamite?'

'He stole it from the engineers when they built the bridge across the channel. It's stored in the fridge at the restaurant along with the detonators,' said Henry.

'That's a smart place to store dynamite.'

'Rudolph fishes out west and starts before sunrise. My guess is he'll pass us on his way home,' said Henry.

They sat in the sun and waited until Rudolph's boat appeared on the horizon. Rudolph throttled back when he reached them and used his hands to signal a good catch; he drifted past and opened the throttle.

'He blasted a full load, packed up tight in those iceboxes,' said Henry, 'the dead fish he left floating on the reef can attract sharks but they won't bother us at White Horse. The best place to see sharks is in the channel under the bridge where great hammerheads hang about the pontoons.' Henry fixed lead weights on his diving belt to go down fast and tied a thin knife round his neck with a leather thong.

'They won't attack us with that to frighten them off,' said Jayce.

'Use it to gut the fish we catch - it's razor sharp,' he passed a knife and diving belt to Jayce, 'great hammerheads sometimes eat each other when they get hungry.'

'That's a consolation,' said Jayce.

They dived for a while then took a breather.

'You speared a decent grouper,' said Henry.

'Beginners luck.'

'Sharks sense underwater vibrations when a fish is hurt,' said Henry.

'You said don't worry about sharks.'

'Right, but with a head shot there are no vibrations and no chance of sharks,' said Henry, 'aim for the head and if sharks still turn up, local fishermen say screaming underwater scares them off.'

'Screaming won't be a problem.'

Jayce kicked for the seabed but surfaced before Henry could join him.

'There's a monster in a cave down there.'

'Could be the light fooled you?' said Henry.

'No, look in the cave where the coral heap joins the main reef.'

'Let me check it out.'

Henry dived from the boat, dragged himself into the cave and let his eyes adjust to the dimness. There was something in the gloom and he pushed further in. When it took shape, he stared into the mouth of a huge fish with jagged teeth. This was big enough to keep the Frenchman going for weeks. Henry kicked for the surface and climbed onto the deck next to Jayce.

'You were right, it's a monster.'

'What is it?'

'I heard fishermen talk about something called a jewfish - some kind of freak grouper or sea bass that live in caves. It has to be one of those and this baby must weigh eight hundred pounds,' said Henry.

'Can we spear it?'

'I don't know,' Henry paused, 'but it's a big prize to give the Frenchman and a real challenge for us. To stand any chance we need a head shot with both spears. Let me think how that can happen.'

Jayce burned for danger but how would he react at the kill? There were bad vibes, which was a weak place for a hit man to start from and Henry was uneasy.

Henry said, 'we shoot at the same time to have a hope of killing it.'

'Fine.'

'You go to the right in the cave and I swim to the left. Pull in close and shoot when I stick up a thumb.'

'OK.'

Henry said, 'hyperventilate for ten seconds then go.' The men stood side-by-side breathing fiercely to pump up their blood oxygen and jumped into the sea.

They went down fast but Jayce couldn't get near enough for a shot and they resurfaced.

'Go down alone and try to get closer,' said Henry, 'he won't move.'

'We didn't spook him.'

'Because he never saw a man before,' Henry said then Jayce dived underwater.

After a minute, Jayce surfaced and climbed on the boat, 'I touched him and saw those teeth close up.'

'Stay away from them when you shoot. Now hyperventilate and we do it for real.'

They knew where to go and it was easy to get in place fast. Henry raised the thumb on his left hand and they fired into the head of the jewfish. Then it went wrong and the fish took off from the cave in a straight line taking both spear guns with his power and weight. The force spun Jayce round and he groped to find the cave entrance. Outside of the cave, the jewfish stopped six feet away, dying in whorls of blood. But it was still alive when the first great hammerhead rammed it and then a second who smashed in with terrific force. The sharks went into their blood frenzy. They must have been close all the time and Jayce knew he was going to die because there was no way past them out of the cave. He cared very much about the way it would happen.

Jayce was fading without oxygen but death in the cave was better than ripping teeth. The hammerheads worried the jewfish to bone and the sea was dark with blood stoking their frenzy. Henry said scream at sharks because they don't like underwater vibrations. Jayce had no breath to scream but made a choice about dying. He pulled his gutting knife from the sheath round his neck to slice his wrists. But sharks would scent blood and rip his flesh while he was alive. It must be an artery cut in the throat and he knew that worked. Strength was ebbing away and it needed a proper stroke. He pulled the skin on his neck tight, and went for a fast slice but something locked his wrist. The sharks had reached him and he opened his eyes in horror.

It was Henry pressing a mouthpiece in his hand. He'd brought the air tank and Jayce hadn't noticed Henry had gone to get the cylinder from the boat. Never once thought about him and now he was breathing again. Lungs full of delicious air and his eyes focused. They shared the mouthpiece in the cave until the frenzy calmed outside.

The sharks left when their meal was stripped clean; ungracious to the last. Dark torpedoes looking for another dinner party on the reef. Henry pointed to the surface and they swam up to the boat. On the deck, Jayce touched the left side of his neck where the blade had pressed.

'Thanks for the oxygen,' said Jayce.

'That's OK.'

'You got to the surface quick after we fired.'

'When the fish took off I hung on to the gun for a couple of seconds and it dragged me out of the cave. The sharks must've been around but I floated to the surface and they didn't notice,' said Henry.

'They chewed it to nothing.'

'You were stuck in the cave and the tank was a last way out.'

'I tried to kill myself.'

'I saw.'

'Another second and it was done.'

'Yeah.'

'Cutting your own throat is a bad way to die,' said Jayce.

'A bad way,' said Henry.

They passed north of Beef Island, gutted their meagre load of fish and packed the fillets in an icebox. Henry clamped on the lid and Jayce threw the guts over the side.

'Italia wants to hear The Doctor preach tonight,' said Henry.

'You'll enjoy hearing a moral expert deliver God's word.'

'The Doctor gives me pills,' said Henry.

'Doctors do that.'

'These are contraceptive pills for women.'

'You won't get pregnant,' said Jayce.

'They were sent here by mistake and a ton of them are stored at the hospital. The Doctor tries this weird experiment using me as a male guinea pig. It could've worked but I saw him shelling tablets out of a packet for me and looked at the wrapping. They got flushed away but he thinks I take them.'

'You were lucky.'

'And his bible stuff?' said Henry.

'He went to theological college as a kid and was thrown out,' said Jayce, 'now religion's his shield.'

'Whatever's happened to him in life must be hell to live with,' said Henry.

'Sooner or later, everybody who deals with him gets hurt. His drinking and shame are defended by religion and a high protector guards his back,' said Jayce, 'one day he knows he'll pay for things.'

'Like I said, his life must be hell,' said Henry.

'But he is a qualified doctor,' said Jayce.

*

They motored to the jetty where Italia waited to land their fish. Henry sent Jayce home while he cleaned up the boat and handed the ice box to Italia to put in the restaurant fridge. He slipped into the sea to check the propeller and felt around to see if the blades were snagged with weed but they were clear. When he used the piles of the jetty as a foothold to climb out he stepped on a sea urchin and its barbed spines pierced deep into his left foot.

Henry scrambled onto the flat boards of the jetty and called for Italia and she ran back from the kitchen. She took his weight on her shoulder and he limped to his bedroom. Henry stripped naked and lay on the bed while Italia washed his foot and tried to pull out the spines with metal tweezers. They broke where the metal clamped.

'There is another way that can help.'

'Do it,' said Henry choking back his pain.

Italia crouched at the end of the bed and put her mouth onto the sole of his foot where most spines were concentrated and began to suck. Occasionally she managed to extract one and spat it out. Pain and pleasure. One caused the other.

'Italia.'

'Yes,' she looked from the end of the bed to his erection and went to him and her jet hair cascading over his belly but he pulled her beside him. She fumbled out of her dress.

'I need to be inside you,' and he entered her at once.

*

Henry's thoughts returned to the present when The Doctor came in with a hypodermic syringe.

'This won't hurt old son,' he inserted the needle gently into the sole of Henry's foot.

'I feel faint,' said Henry.

'You can't faint lying down,' but the pilot was white-faced and clammy with sweat, 'the bugger's conked out, give him some oxygen nurse,' The Doctor said. She pulled over an oxygen cylinder and put a breather mask on Henry's face.

'Never seen anything like it,' he took Henry's wrist, 'pulse down in his boots...most odd.'

Henry pushed the mask away and groaned, 'I feel awful.'

'You look awful, lie back and relax. The worst is over.'

'Needles and me don't mix.'

'The next bit is painless.'

'If you say so,' Henry took a deep breath and the colour returned to his face, 'get me a damp cloth nurse.'

'Sure,' she went to the next room and turned on a tap.

'Doc.'

'Yes.'

'Your nephew,' said Henry.

'What about him?'

'The oxygen mask reminded me about him on the reef yesterday.'

'Jayce said you saved his life,' said The Doctor.

'Not quite so dramatic, but listen to me while the nurse is out.'

'Calm down.'

'He hates the army. He hates what The Queen stands for,' said Henry.

'Relax.'

'He talked plenty about The Queen opening her bridge. For some reason he wants to see her do it,' said Henry.

'The Queen is his boss.'

'Plenty of things he said were odd and he dives like a madman,' said Henry.

'Jayce is impulsive but thanks for keeping him alive.'

'I mean *mad* like *crazy* Doc.'

'His mother was highly strung too. If you feel better, we'll start.'

'Yeah, he told me how his mother died. Forget it - go ahead,' Henry said when the nurse came in with his cloth.

The spines were concentrated in the centre of Henry's left foot and The Doctor removed a lot of flesh to get to reach the barbed ends. The nurse took Henry's hand but he seemed to be asleep. The Doctor used silver nitrate to cauterise the wound. Henry would have a lot of pain when the anaesthetic wore off. There were more pills available to help.

'Put on a dressing and you can go nurse,' he pulled off his gown as she left.

'What now doc?'

'There'll be pain.'

'How much?' said Henry.

'A bit when you walk.'

'I need to walk,' said Henry.

'There are tablets to make it easier.'

'My schedule is busy,' said Henry.

'Flying or social?'

'Both.'

The Doctor helped him to sit up, 'your social life is dynamite.'

'Doc, your nephew has fragile nerves.'

'He's a soldier.'

'But always tense...other people see it, not just me.'

'This place is full of gossips. Jayce is relaxing in the sun.'

'He's wound up.'

'Perhaps island life makes him edgy?'

'There's more than that.'

'Tittle-tattle,' said The Doctor.

'No.'

'It's his holiday; there's nothing more.'

Henry said, 'Jayce hates you,' and raised his hand to stop The Doctor's protest, 'he told me about his mother and I see the way he watches you, he said you were too drunk to help his mother when she killed herself. I understand about revenge.'

'What do you mean, revenge?' The Doctor shouted.

'You need to figure it out,' said Henry.

'I'm his uncle,' The Doctor shouted louder.

'Yeah,' said Henry, 'but I know how revenge works.'

'Nonsense,' The Doctor calmed down.

Henry said, 'when he fired that spear at dinner was it aimed at you or the picture of The Queen it hit? Believe me, Jayce is disturbed.'

'It was an accident. Let's see if you can walk out of here?' said The Doctor.

*

20

1964 Beirut

Icy walked along the Corniche watched by Mossad agents. The Mediterranean sparkled on his left side but Israeli watchers hid in buildings to his right. The main road separated him from them and Icy knew there were guns trained on him as a precaution. Michael was Icy's controller and liked to control things. Michael followed Icy's progress along the Corniche by moving from window to window in the Hotel Normandie. Icy carried a Persian rug fastened tight into a linen bag such as tourists bought in carpet shops and ambled along the promenade enjoying the views. There were a lot of ships in the harbour. Last year *the Dolmotova* sailed Kim Philby, the British traitor, out of Lebanon to Russia after his final drink in the Normandie Hotel. Beirut was a city full of spies. Michael ghosted across the Normandie bar to the front window when Icy passed the main entrance.

It was surprising that his small rug grew heavy and Icy was glad to reach the marina yacht club because the sun was hot. The concierge controlled the flow of people from his ornate desk in the lobby. The concierge's brother worked as a professional beggar outside Icy's carpet shop and he beckoned Icy to the front of the line as a favoured visitor.

'Your guests are here and the Mezze is served but I put a shade over your table. The roof gets hot even with a breeze and its keeps the other tables clear of you. They seem a nice couple, and will appreciate the merchandise you bring them,' the concierge nodded at the bag, 'the Dabke dancers go on soon. Sit close to hear your friends over the music.'

'Others relatives will visit to see the dance,' said Icy.

'Four men have arrived. There isn't space by your table but you'll see them standing near the pool.'

'Michael will come with a present for you,' said Icy.

'He likes to cover that door. It's the only way down from the roof terrace.'

The line of people behind, were impatient and Icy walked up the stairs with his rug to the open-air roof of the yacht club. Before he went into the sunlight, he made the shape of a bird with his fingers as a reminder to be vigilant. In the shade was the table allocated by the concierge with food being served to a man and woman. The waiter left when Icy joined them. The man wore sunglasses and she smoked a cigarette. There was a third chair and he went over, shook hands and sat down.

'Eat while the food is fresh. We'll talk business when the music starts,' said Icy.

'I can't resist Shanklish,' said the man, 'this one is made from sheep's milk.'

'Ach,' said the woman, 'but covered in Aleppo pepper and thyme. How can cheese like that be an aphrodisiac?'

'When you eat it with fuul, the Lebanese say it fires emotion,' said Icy, 'keep the two separate and there's calm.'

'Quiet when separate,' said the man, 'like Palestinian and Jew.'

The band played a tablah, hand drum and rikk, and tambourine. The dancers lined up on the dance area boarded over for the show. Icy looked across the empty floor to the shoreline of Beirut and the great sweep of the bay up to St George's Marina. The Corniche was broken in places but the road along the seafront was quiet in the afternoon and a few taxis worked their trade near The Normandie Hotel. The music was still too soft for their business conversation.

Icy said, 'Michael would like this food.'

The woman said, 'don't tempt fate. He would eat it all and want more. He's fat but his mind is quick.'

'When the mijwiz clarinet starts the dancers will take the floor,' Icy said.

'Michael likes baba ghanouj,' said the man, 'but if he lived on egg plant he'd be thin like me.'

The woman said, 'I wonder if Michael has ever been really hungry or if any of us has?'

'I have,' said Icy.

The mijwiz trilled and the Dabke line started a foot-stomping show representing the mending of village roofs with mud after winter.

Icy said, 'we have enough noise to talk but first let me present this,' he unbuttoned the linen bag and laid out an exquisite Persian rug by the side of the table. 'I'm a carpet salesman trying to interest you in my wares.'

'It's not my taste,' said the woman.

'And a shit price,' said the man, and then whispered, 'what were you doing with your hands?'

'I made the shape of a bird,' said Icy.

'Why?' said the woman, lighting another cigarette.

'Birds fly and see everything. We talk and see nothing. I try to think like a bird and see everything, while we talk,' said Icy.

'The rug is still a shit price,' said the man who played his part well.

Icy looked disappointed and the woman said, 'leave it on the floor, it might grow on me,' and murmured to her partner, 'tell him what we came to talk about. Keep close.'

'When you get to my age the past is bigger than the future,' the man said to Icy.

'Save time and tell him about which slice of the past interests us,' the woman said.

Icy said, 'keep it short. Too much conversation can put you in a coffin in Beirut. Talk fast and when I roll up the carpet your fill goes in it. Remember, somebody or other is watching us in this place. I'm clean in the city so keep it looking like business. After I leave, get the bill, pay for the meal as if you were pissed at the cost and take your time before you go. The dance will last another hour. Now talk.'

For fifteen minutes, the man told him about their German SS target in the Caribbean and the implication for Israel if Icy could find his stolen goods. Israeli intelligence was not sure what the German looked like or where his stuff might be hidden. Killing a war criminal was fine, but uncover his secrets first and then do it. This briefing was for Icy alone. Michael had no details and Icy was Israel's solo agent if he accepted the job.

'You guys are kinda short on facts. How reliable is your source of information?'

'It came from an American woman who gave it for free,' the man said.

'How come you trust free information - nine times out of ten, free equals worthless?'

'She was Jewish and scored high with our evaluation team,' said the woman.

'Yeah,' Icy said, 'but she might have blabbed to others. You know how Jews like to talk.'

'So look out for competition,' said the woman.

They waited for an answer while Icy thought. He took his time.

'My answer is yes to the assignment, but only if you cut me loose. No contact from Israel and cover for the operation is my choice without surveillance to knock it off balance. You won't know my cover and don't try to figure it out. I take a personal hit man with me but he's my boy to pay off afterwards. Down the line, my link is Michael. I deal with him and people he controls when it gets to the finale. A sniff of Mossad scouts like you got me ringed with today on the Corniche, and I run. Set things up and forget about my hitter and me for a couple of years while we go to sleep.'

Icy kneeled to roll up his rug and the man bent down to help. Each took an end to keep it straight to fit in the linen bag. At halfway the man took off his jacket in the heat and as he put it on the chair, slipped out a tube from the sleeve and palmed it nicely into the centre of the rug. When it was rolled tight, the man helped Icy slide the rug into its linen bag.

'Thanks for the Mezze,' Icy said, 'my call next time.'

'We can be patient if you bring us the goods. I want this guy strung up but his merchandise comes first in our priorities. Get his stuff even if you lose him,' the man said.

Icy said, 'keep Michael available in Beirut while I wind up my end of the operation here and arrange travel. In ten days, we'll be gone and then it goes quiet for up to a couple of years. Stay patient.'

The woman chain-smoked another cigarette, 'Michael says you know how to live alone with secrets. Alone is hard but he says you can do it. Right now, is an opportunity to get something priceless for us and that's why we risk cutting you loose with no control. Bring us the stuff we want and our dreams come true. You're on your own till then.'

'You got plenty of hotshot agents...why me?'

'You have special qualifications. The information's in there,' she tapped the rug.

'Pay the fucking bill,' said Icy.

The man laughed and swiped at a wasp buzzing his head and lost his shades. Icy looked into one eye but the other was just a socket and then he put the shades back again. Nobody saw and the woman was looking in her purse for money.

'Check the total and play for time while I get a start,' and Icy got up with his rug. They shook hands and he went over to the door leading from the roof area. As he moved off, four men closed in around the couple. The woman called a waiter to bring the bill.

At the concierge's desk, Michael was gone and Icy walked out by the sea. Along the Corniche, he felt the eyes on him. Icy knew this was as high level as it got with that man and woman who'd swallowed his terms. So far, he counted six Mossad bystanders and there was probably double that number in place. The man and woman were important, and that made him important. They said he could work his hit man and let him retire but Mossad never put hitters out to grass, just under it. And, who the fuck was the German in the Caribbean and what were his secrets that could agitate the top brass of Israel? Icy's special qualifications for the job were inside the rug in his linen bag.

*

21

The Caribbean - St Croix

Monday 12.00 - 21st February 1966

What pissed Henry off most was flying dirty laundry. Clean bags smelled OK but the dirty ones stank of old food from restaurants and blood from hospitals. There was a special escape hatch in the cockpit because laundry was piled up to the roof of the cabin and there was no way to the door. What bright mother thought anyone would get out of an escape hatch buried under a mountain of laundry? His foot exploded with pain but there was a clean load to fly back. Icy didn't tell him in Beirut he'd ferry dirty tablecloths and bed sheets in the Caribbean. The Doctor didn't tell him the level of agony to expect in his foot. The Doctor was big on deceit and Henry needed to check some facts when he drove him home tonight.

Henry dropped the gear, pushed the propellers to fully fine and turned on final approach to St Croix's Alexander Hamilton Airport. He opted for a three-point landing but the tail hit the runway before the main wheels and he swung all over the concrete like a low-time student pilot. It all looked easy when he watched the flights land at Beirut airport as a kid. It all sounded easy in Beirut, when Icy told him how he could learn to fly if he really wanted to. Icy made things seem easy but Henry eventually understood that Icy never let things happen by chance. Not then and not now.

Nobody gave a shit if he wrote off the old Beech. There were hundreds of them used as island hoppers and Icy's linen rental company bought this one to fly laundry. They cost next to nothing. Laundry was big business. Who would guess people wanted to rent so much linen and towels that an aeroplane was needed to fly the stuff. Icy had his fingers in plenty of things that made money. He said money was their best cover.

'Stay where you are man,' the truck driver shouted up to Henry, 'there isn't much and I'll fling it on real quick.'

'OK,' that saved fifteen minutes and the load wasn't due until the next day.

'Tower from Eighty Juliet.'

'Go ahead.'

'Ready in five minutes. File me a VFR flight plan to Tortola.'

'Wilco. Start and taxi at your discretion. Call ready for take-off.'

The driver left and he fired up the R-985 engines and rolled across the apron to the runway. This tail wheel Beech D18S was not friendly but he enjoyed the test of skill on take-off and landing. It was easy to ground loop and that was embarrassing at busy airports.

'Eighty Juliet - cleared for take-off, VFR Tortola,' the controller said and Henry dropped in the tail wheel lock and eased open the throttles. VFR was Visual Flight Rules and the afternoon sky was clear when Henry set course for Tortola. He levelled out and thought about Karl's conversation when he flew him on Friday. Remember what he said. Think what he meant.

How Karl struggled onto the Apache wing with his breath coming fast and beads of sweat on his face. Funny, he never looked at Gunter as they taxied out but talked when they were in the cruise.

'Do you have you a trip scheduled when you get to New York?'

'Tomorrow,' said Karl.

'You won't make it.'

'The airline has stand-ins they can use and I want out of here,' said Karl.

'Gunter was rough other times.'

'He got worse and it stinks on the island.'

'It stinks for me too.'

'If you come to New York stop by,' Karl took out a notebook and scribbled his address and phone number.

Henry put the paper in his shirt pocket, 'OK, but I'm a women-only-guy.'

Karl laughed, 'what a waste.'

'You sound better,' said Henry.

'Things get better as we fly off.'

'Stop thinking about what happened here.'

'There's other history with us two.'

'We all rake up stuff from the past; move on,' said Henry.

'Forgetting the past is tough with Gunter in the frame.'

'Who else grabs your attention on the island?'

'Sneaky people who live there grab my attention,' said Karl.

'I see dull people.'

'Dull people look the same as sneaky people.'

'Like, who is sneaky - hold it while I turn?' Henry pulled the Apache into a sixty-degree bank at a thousand feet to turn downwind, parallel to the runway at St Thomas. The G force pulled Karl's cheeks down until he looked like a clown with sad eyes. He levelled off and Karl's face was normal again. A woman in the back seat started to cry when he pulled the 2G turn but Karl was used to his manoeuvres.

'Jayce wants Gunter. You can see that, and Gunter likes soldiers.'

'Gunter screws around.'

'Jayce is a soldier,' said Karl, 'and he's a sneaky guy.'

Henry turned onto a tight base leg so the passengers on the inside of the turn looked down at the sea. The woman in the back seat whimpered in fear.

Karl went on, 'Jayce isn't the only sneaky guy around but none of them will worry me in New York.'

'Are you and Gunter Americans?'

'Yeah, from immigrant stock.'

'What're you saying?' Henry pulled the Apache onto final approach with a tight turn and straightened up at five hundred feet. The control tower cleared him to land.

'Nothing,' Karl was defensive and stared ahead at the runway.

Henry changed the subject, 'find another guy in New York,'

'I did that for entertainment.'

'You're safe in the city.'

'It doesn't work that way with Gunter.'

'He'll forget and you'll get over it.'

'He won't forget our birthday. Yeah, it's weird our birthdays are on the same day. Every year we get together then. This time he organised a special present for me.'

'Maybe Gunter dumps Jayce,' said Henry.

'Whatever he does, me and him go way back and he'll come for our birthday.'

'Where to?'

'New York. But now I got a bad feeling about him that gurgles up.'

'When is this joint birthday?'

'On Thursday next week; February the twenty fourth.'

22

The Caribbean - Tortola

Monday 15.30 - 21st February 1966

When Henry got to the restaurant, the Frenchman was out and the kitchen deserted. He rummaged through the fridge and found some cheese on top of Rudolph's dynamite box. He made a sandwich and ate it looking across Trellis Bay. Italia moved behind him and when she touched his neck, Henry came out of his chair in a crouch.

'Don't creep.'

'Sorry...are you staying?' said Italia.

'For a few minutes before I go into town.'

'Come back to me tonight.'

'Perhaps,' said Henry.

She kneeled down in front of him and looked up into his face, pressing her fingers together.

'It is only because I care that I ask. You do not look after yourself,' Italia spoke the words carefully with a French accent.

'You know the rules and I run alone,' he ran his thumb along her oriental cheekbones.

'I am yours whenever you wish,' said Italia.

'Later.'

'There is time.'

'Yes,' he sighed, 'always time for that.'

Italia stood up to her full height and leaned forward to kiss him but he held her away. She bent to reach his lips and her open blouse showed perfect breasts and her nipples were erect. Henry smiled. After they made love, she put on a demure shift sent by her mother. Dressed in penance to atone for the sin she had committed. Henry knew no woman like her yet she was still a girl.

It would be easy to leave without her devotion and Henry looked for selfish motives in Italia to justify his exit but there was no flaw. Walking away from other women was straightforward. Women meant trouble for Henry.

'Henry.'

'Yes.'

'I do love you,' said Italia.

'Not love.'

'I know you do not love me and I do not expect it but I do love you and you make me very happy when you stay with me,' said Italia.

'We fuck.'

'It is not like that for me,' said Italia.

'I'm grateful.'

'Nothing more is asked,' said Italia.

'Get married and I'll go someplace.' Henry saw her eyes fill with tears, 'enjoy our time now.'

Italia whispered through her tears, 'I will not hold you back but please stay with me until you go.'

'No promises,' said Henry.

'Can you assist me about something else Henry?'

'Of course,' he slipped an arm round her shoulder and pulled her onto his lap so that her head lay on his chest.

'I wanted to tell you on Saturday morning but you said it was too early to speak.'

*

On Saturday, Henry woke at dawn to sounds filtering through the ceiling above his bed. He nudged Italia awake, and she rolled away.

'It is still not light,' she said.

'I heard the Frenchman move in the roof,' said Henry.

'He goes to use his telescope,' said Italia.

'What does he look at?'

'He looks at nonsense things. He told me Gunter stayed on the cay one night by the lime tree,' said Italia. They heard the Frenchman return to his bedroom, 'he can see all directions from the lantern window in the roof.'

Henry went up the stairs and turned the telescope to the airport which was asleep in the last traces of night. Slowly he scanned over the bridge and up the mountainside to Old Sarah's shack. Gunter's face was white and stark, framed in the empty window of the shack. Henry watched for thirty minutes then went to his room.

*

Henry said, 'I remember Saturday, but it's Monday today,' he stroked her hair, 'what were you going to tell me on Saturday that's stayed secret for two days?'

'I am going to have a baby,' she pressed her face hard into his chest.

'Oh.'

*

23

The Caribbean - Tortola

Monday 17.30 - 21st February 1966

By early evening The Doctor was drunk and sat with Snoopy on the bar terrace. The dog squeezed tight against her master and he stroked her ears. Evening drinkers trickled in as businesses closed. At the side of The Doctor's chair was a bucket of water with small fish swimming in it. Old Sarah sold him the fish to put in the underground water tank at his house. She said they were guppy fish and ate mosquito larvae that bred in the tank. The Doctor believed Sarah but needed confirmation from Henry. He also needed confirmation of the pain level in Henry's foot to see if his special tablets worked.

From the terrace, he saw that Gunter's shop was still open and hoped it would close soon. Jayce stretched out on a lounger with a drink, enjoying the late sunshine. The Doctor dangled his fingers in the bucket of fishes and spoke quietly to the dog.

'You see Snoops, certainty is not enough for the powers in Whitehall. After all the information we've supplied, they request a final nugget about our man. We could ask Gunter to show us what they want to see and he'd vanish to a new paradise. Two wasted years stalking him here. And the powers want me to give them evidence after the event. Photographic evidence Snoops. There's no time to send it but they want to cover their bums whatever it costs. Telling Jayce what he must do, will be unpleasant. Are you on my side old girl?'

The dog raised her head when a waiter passed carrying a plate of fish for a customer. Snoopy wriggled at the memory-scent of her fish breakfasts. The Doctor gently pulled her ears and she calmed down.

'The Chief says "*use our soldier to confirm one last detail and we'll give you the go-ahead from Blighty.*" My last job is as a whore-messenger. Order your nephew to prostitute himself for the good of Britain.'

He agitated the water in the bucket so it spilled over the rim onto the terrace and Snoopy looked up in alarm.

'Quite right to get anxious old girl, we don't want to lose our fishes,' he pushed the bucket out of reach and the dog settled back. A cloud sat over the distant mountain peak and it might be raining on the summit. The Doctor had followed Gunter up the mountain during his time on the island, but never to the top. Mostly he followed Gunter to a safe distance from Sarah's shack. The Doctor paid well to buy information from Old Sarah and knew everything about Gunter except the mystery they craved to unravel in Whitehall. He didn't know where Gunter's secrets were hidden but Jayce was the honeytrap to discover that. Jayce -

his nephew whose mother cut her own throat. Jayce - who blamed The Doctor for her death.

'Two hundred dollars is a generous sum for guppy fish Snoops but occasionally dollars aren't enough. Final proof is what Whitehall desire and commands me to sell Jayce. Sarah can't fix this particular piece of evidence for money so we use the honeytrap route with no guarantee we find Gunter's stockpile.' Snoopy rubbed her nose against his hand when The Doctor's other friends came in with Gunter.

*

Gunter's stillness fascinated The Doctor and he concentrated hard. The Doctor's power of observation was at its best. Alcohol depressed most people's nervous system but for him it provided insights before unconsciousness set in. Lucid visions came into his mind. Usually by first light the next day, he forgot his visions but not always. Perhaps only important insights were retained. It disturbed him what he remembered on some mornings. That lucidity was in him now and he vowed to remember at least one thing tomorrow. He ignored the conversation at the table, kept his eyes on Gunter, and watched the muscles in his arms move when he raised his glass. Gunter leaned back, clasped his hands behind his head and showed the upper part of both arms.

There was a burn scar on the inside of his left bicep. It was a rectangular shape that was too symmetrical to be other than deliberate and too perfect to be accidental. There was no other flaw on his skin and no scar on the right bicep. The Doctor sipped his drink and promised to remember. The time was approaching for Henry to drive him home. This special time didn't last and was precious to him and what he worked towards each day with alcohol. Gunter was distracted by the other drinkers when The Doctor closed in on Jayce. His spectacles slipped to the end of his nose and he tipped his head back to stop them falling.

'Dear boy,' The Doctor's face was inches away and his voice a whisper but he tugged insistently and Jayce moved closer, 'the effects of acid are singular.'

'Acid?' said Jayce.

'Concentrated acid. Don't see many people burned with it these days,' said The Doctor.

'No.'

'It's interesting…look at the inside of Gunter's left arm when he sits back in his chair. There's a section of acid-burned skin, which is very precise. Twenty-five years ago, it was fashionable to have your blood group tattooed there if you were pure Aryan SS. No blood transfusions into Aryan bodies allowed except from other pure Aryans in warfare you see. No racially tainted blood to be introduced into pure Aryans was their way of thinking and Hitler supported that theory. After the war, it became fashionable to have the tattoo burned off and the evidence removed that you were Aryan SS. War crimes hysterics and all that. Stupid really because the evidence just changed to an acid scar. We need a photograph of Gunter's scar and his face together in one shot. He'd need to be undressed. My masters insist.' His words faded and he flopped in the chair exhausted with the effort. He took a final look at Gunter who was locked on Jayce and with the players etched in his mind, The Doctor slid away. Henry listened to the speech from his chair behind them. When The Doctor slumped into oblivion, Henry helped him to his feet and they shuffled out.

*

24

The Caribbean - San Juan

Tuesday 11.00 - 22nd February 1966

All that day Icy stayed with Henry. They talked and watched the rollers come in fast off the Atlantic. Controller and killer stood on the wall of the old Spanish fort named El Morro that guarded the entrance to San Juan harbour.

Icy said, 'one day they gonna have the world surfing championships here in Puerto Rico. Those waves are bigger down west of the island. Blue water comes rolling in big and high for the boards...lotta kids down there...I go down to watch some.'

'You're not interested in surfing.'

'I can't stand it. I go down to watch the young pussy. You should've come with me.'

'I got troubles enough without kids at the beach,' said Henry.

'I love this island,' Icy said, 'it's got everything that agrees with me and the sun shines all year. I do good business and gotta nice place.'

'That's your cover Icy. You're a crook and a pervert and they like crooks and perverts here. Your Israeli boys sure gave you a good story.'

With a pained look Icy said, 'the cover is mine. Those jerks in Israel could never figure this out. You harsh with your assessment.'

'You're my boss. Crook and pervert is all right.'

'Now we eat a last meal at the club.'

'OK.'

'Let's walk through the old town.'

'The streets are dangerous there,' said Henry.

'Sure, but like in Beirut, let danger seep through your skin until you smell it early.'

'You walk in Old San Juan and nobody touches you. I go in and get mugged.'

'Connections are important and a lotta people owe me. Stay close kid.'

'How does a Polish Catholic talk like a New York Jew?'

'With a good ear.'

Icy's club was a brothel but everybody called it *The Club* for respectability. When executives phoned to make appointments it sounded fine in the office. There were rules of attendance for the girls. They were in place before nine at night and weren't allowed to leave before dawn. Guests came and went but the girls stayed put.

'How many girls work this place Icy?'

'A few hundred.'

'More than enough for all your dreams.'

'Enough for the dreams of guys that visit and this place does a lotta good,' said Icy, 'those holy persons who yap about these girls want to think again. I do good for the girls.'

'Yeah?'

'I ain't got no direct connection with the joint but the way I see it is this. Ya come here and get free music and good food. They sell guys a bottle of rum for five dollars, which is cost. Ya been fed and boozed-up for less than ten bucks.'

'The girls aren't cheap.'

'Have a heart...ya know where they come from?'

'No.'

'They come from Columbia, they come from Venezuela and they come from Brazil. One thing these dames got in common is they come from respectable families. What they ain't got is two cents to rub together and that means trouble in those places.'

'It means they're poor like they would be anywhere,' said Henry.

'Is different there for a girl when your folks ain't got no money. It means ya ain't gonna get married because ya ain't got a dowry. Ya ain't got a fucking dowry, ya ain't gonna get a husband on earth.'

'How do you save them, Icy?'

'This is how. Young girls desperate for a dowry just to get some lousy punk husband come here for three months - no longer than three months. The work is tiring, but they come here to make a dowry and then they go home with money and get married and be nice respectable wives forever,' said Icy.

'You got some imagination about doing good. What sort of guy wants to marry a girl who turned five tricks a night for three months?'

'That's where it gets smart - hear me. These girls are supposed to be innocents back home. After three months, their agent gives them a nice alibi to take back to South America as happy girls with money. Ain't that doing good?'

Henry said, 'where does an agent come in?'

'The agent has nothing to do with the joint. All he does is organise the girls to come here and fix for them to go home with an alibi.'

'This agent gets paid?'

'Strictly commission.'

'How much?'

'Twenty five percent of what the girl makes and she takes what's left...less her keep and round trip fare,' said Icy.

'Twenty five percent each is a lot.'

'It ain't a lot for doing so much good. Last year I took thirty percent.'

'You mean you're the agent?'

Icy's eyes widened, 'hey...I never told you...sure I must've done.'

'I never knew how much good you did in the world, Icy.'

A steel band struck up on a revolving stage in the *hooking* area. At night it was crowded with girls and punters but now there were only a few daygirls around and it felt empty. Henry liked it calm before a hit and the place suited his mood. One girl moved in but saw Icy and left fast. In daytime, the club was quiet but it was air-conditioned and the food was good. A waitress took their order.

'Suddenly you're a saint busting your ass preaching what's good. Remind me about those five thousand bucks you turned down for us.'

'Some dollars are bad.'

'My contact arranged we fly in at night to a beach on the Dominican Republic and pick up eight guys and fly them back to a beach here. Five grand for one flight ain't bad dollars.'

'It bothered me what happened when they landed,' said Henry.

'This contact meets you and when the eight guys get off he shoots them.'

'That's murder,' said Henry.

'They illegal immigrants. Is doing free work for the government and they gonna come in some other way.'

'It's still murder.'

153

'You're my fucking hit man - murder is your game,' said Icy.

'What'd they say about this setup in Israel?'

'They know what I tell them which is nothing,' said Icy. 'No fucking instruction from Tel Aviv gonna keep you alive. You gotta be in the part for real or a schmuck spots your act and you get dead. Plenty of schmucks out there so string along with Icy and stay in one piece. The next hit is the end of the line kid.'

*

25

The Caribbean - San Juan

Tuesday 13.00 - 22nd February 1966

At full power the vibrating chair caused a loss of vision and Henry eased back on the control. It made him feel sick and shook undigested chunks of food into his mouth. He stopped the chair.

'These chairs make me sick,' said Henry.

'Nobody complained before,' Icy said.

'Nobody complained because they just got invented.'

'You ate too early before the ride.'

'Everybody eats.'

'I ordered ten more chairs,' said Icy.

'Think about tomorrow and cancel the order.'

'There was a deposit.'

'Write it off,' said Henry, 'you won't be around.'

Icy's apartment was over a pastry shop and the smell of bread and cakes was everywhere. Most of the rooms were empty but in one, he'd installed vibrating chairs powered by electric motors. They were America's latest furniture relaxation.

'Try again and lie flat,' Icy said from his chair. His Haitian girlfriend watched them. She wore white panties and sunglasses.

'I never saw a girl so black,' said Henry.

'She's real pretty and crazy for the chairs.'

'Beautiful,' Henry admired the girl's aquiline features.

'This one I keep until she turns nineteen,' Icy said.

'You won't see her birthday so what happens when you leave?'

'I fixed her a cleaning job at the place I buy these chairs and she's gonna love it there.'

'Let me imagine,' said Henry.

At one end of the room, Icy gunned up his chair and sank in the leather cushions. Henry saw the number on his forearm ripple. His girl walked over and Icy got up and she curled on the warm leather and pushed the control lever. On full power, her small breast stayed firm. An illiterate teenager, vibrating at one end of a thirty-foot room. Icy went to a different chair.

Standing between them, Henry sensed her eyes missed nothing from behind the shades. He wanted to talk and pulled the control lever to cut the motor on Icy's chair.

'Hey man,' said Icy.

Henry turned to the girl, 'some coffee please.'

'Un peu de café s'il vous plaît,' Icy said to her and she went to the kitchen. 'I know ya like to talk plenty before a hit.'

'This might be your last chance to hear this, Icy.'

'Talk,' Icy closed the kitchen door.

'Remember that trip I made down islands for lobster?'

'It made money.'

'We land on a beach. Rudolph came for the ride and the fishermen are waiting there with sacks of lobster and load them in the plane while I look around. When they finish I pay the boss his dollars but he takes my arm and calls Rudolph and we go over to where something is lying at the side of the strip. The boss is grateful we buy his lobster and has a present for me. He knows I won't handle his gift and wants Rudolph to help. There's a turtle lying on its back and these guys have left him staring into the sun and he's gone blind. The boss man says this turtle is a gift for me. He knows it's blind but that's what they do when they capture turtles there - lay them on their back staring at the sun. He says the turtle is worth good money and maybe Rudolph keeps the shell and I get the meat. So I say OK not thinking any more of it.'

'Those shells bring good dollars,' said Icy.

'We take off and it's like flying a million cockroaches because all these lobster are fighting and squirming in the gunny sacks. They put the turtle where the front seat was taken out and he's lying on his back with his head turned towards me and staring even though he's blind. Rudolph is behind with the lobster and the turtle watches. He never moves at all and soon I get a funny feeling the turtle can see something, even though he's blind. I get an idea he knows something about me that I don't.'

Icy touched his arm to stop and pulled his chair closer.

'Go on kid.'

'About twenty miles from the island, it comes to me like this Icy. If the turtle knows something about me...and by this time I'm sure the turtle does know something...you know those feelings you get once in a while - so if he does know something I ask myself why don't I know it? How is it I can't figure out what a dumb creature from the sea knows? I shake my head and say who cares. Then it comes to me what the turtle knows.'

'What?'

'It's why he's looking at me like that. He knows I don't care.'

'Why care about a fucking turtle?'

'Wait a minute Icy. He knows I don't care about him, the same way he don't care about what he eats in the sea.'

'That's right.'

'But he knows more.'

'Surprise me kid.'

'He knows I don't care about anything.'

'How the fuck can a turtle know that?'

'Because the turtle was right, I don't care about anything, and your girl just looked at me the same through her shades. She knows the same thing.'

Icy picked up a carton of chocolate milk. He sat close.

'Ya care about screwing all those dames.'

'I care about it for me but not about them,' said Henry.

'Ya the chauffeur to The Doctor - that's caring.'

'It amuses me but I don't really care.'

'So where does this story go?'

'I watched the turtle and ran through what I cared about and didn't find anything. I thought hard but there was nothing.'

'Kid, ya my hitter. Caring isn't needed in that field.'

'Let me finish Icy.'

Icy put his fingers to his lips, 'stop there and tell me if I figure some place in your story?'

'Hear me out.'

'I'm listening,' said Icy.

'They unload the lobster in Tortola and drive off but leave the turtle with me and Rudolph. By this time, I can hardly breathe with those blind eyes looking at me and I need to get away from them. We put him in the truck and drive to the quay in town where they hang the big fish off the charter boats. Rudolph calls over a few people to look at it. Gunter is there and says he'll buy the shell. Rudolph gets his machete and fish knife. I say how about we put the poor bastard back in the water but they all laugh and think it's a joke.'

'See, ya cared about the turtle.'

'No, I felt guilty and went over to him. He opened his beak a few times like he was trying to say something and I bent over to hear. It's when I saw you Icy.'

'Me?'

'Your face looking up at me - don't ask me to explain. And I thought what the fuck is going on, but I swear it was your face down there on the quay.'

Henry paced about the room.

'So, I try again, with, "let's put the poor bastard back in the water," but Rudolph arrives with the steel and I hear Gunter say to the boy - under his breath but I hear him just the same - he says, "five bucks you let me do it," and the boy nods and gives him the machete. Now there's nothing to stop him. I'm three feet from the turtle looking at your face. Sweating and doing nothing, then Gunter kneels down and says to me, "killing is often a favour," then he looks into those blind eyes like he's in ecstasy and takes one swipe and cuts the turtle's head off. To me it's like your head was cut off Icy.'

'Motherfucker.'

The girl padded barefoot from the kitchen and Icy said, 'get lost,' and she went out.

'All those hits and I didn't feel anything and this turtle screws me up.'

'Yeah,' said Icy.

'Rudolph kneels down with his knife and cuts the turtle open and pulls his guts out and drops them on the jetty and you know what?'

'Go on kid.'

'His heart is still beating. Gunter sees it, and picks it up throbbing in his hand. He says, "in all my time I never saw that with anybody," and throws it back with the rest of the guts.'

'Ya sure he said, I never saw that with *anybody*?'

'He said *anybody.* That's what I'm trying to tell you - he said *anybody*. So, he steps close to the turtle's head and you know what, the fucking head is still alive and snaps at him and the beak takes a hold of his trousers. There's him jumping about trying to get rid of it and kicking his leg but it won't let go until finally he pulls it off with a piece of cloth still in its beak, and throws the head out to sea.'

'You said it was dead.'

'I know it was dead but a fisherman told me he knew about a turtle's head being cut off and still biting things. Same thing as chickens sometimes do. But that doesn't matter. It's what he said I wanted to tell you, and how I felt when it was your face lying on the quay. I cared about that.'

'Good to know kid.'

'After he threw the head in the sea he looked at me and I never saw a face like that on a man.'

'You mean he was scared?'

'No, he was crazy-mad because that turtle took hold of him. Imagine how he'd be with people who crossed him?'

'Imagine?'

The girl came out of the kitchen and went to the chair at the end of the room.

'She must've got bored,' Icy said, 'you should try her for an hour.'

'Forget the girl, there's more.'

'Go on.'

'You know what happens on Tortola with The Queen tomorrow?' Henry said.

'Yeah.'

'Everybody is hyped-up about it on the island because The Queen and her husband are coming to open the bridge across the channel.'

'The Queen of Britain and her King?'

'He's called The Duke of Edinburgh but they open the bridge at noon.'

'Why d'ya figure tomorrow is important?'

'Early Saturday morning I'm playing with the Frenchman's telescope in the roof window and I see Gunter on the mountain. The day before his boyfriend tells me about their birthday reunion that happens every year without fail and I put two and two together.'

'Tell me what *four* you figured out,' said Icy and Henry told him.

Icy said, 'it stacks up so we do it tomorrow. But the hit ain't enough. I got more than that to weigh up. I got stuff to find.'

*

26

1939 Warsaw

Icy's mother was a widow called Anna Czeberowski. She came from a family of Polish Catholics. Her son's name was Ignacy and Anna prayed for him every day. Being the single mother of a child became harder when Hitler turned his attention to Poland and Anna fell in love with a man called Dudel Warski who was Jewish. Dudel gave her son Ignacy, the diminutive name of Icy and it stuck. Eventually, even Anna called him Icy.

It was difficult for Jew and Catholic to marry but they did and afterwards made plans when Hitler's ambitions were clear. Dudel had a gentile friend in the Warsaw registry who stole papers that might be useful. He took one set showing Dudel and Anna as man and wife and another set showing Anna as the widow of Jan Czeberowski. As things turned out this was fortunate because a respectable marriage to Dudel became less important than not being Jewish. The difference lay between guaranteed death and probable death.

When invasion was certain, Dudel explained the situation to Anna and broke his own heart. He told her about the danger of being a Jewish wife when the German army came to Warsaw. Jews all over Europe were fleeing from Hitler but he had nowhere to go. Not only that but she didn't look Jewish and nor did Icy. Dudel insisted she use her widow's papers. Icy and her were blond with pale skin. The gamble began and the stake was life.

Occupied Warsaw was ruled by fear and German policies were brutal. When storm troopers kicked in their door Dudel pretended to be a servant and tried to divert attention from mother and son hidden in the bedroom. There was a shot and Dudel cried out. Soldiers dragged Anna and Icy down the stairs past the body of Dudel sprawled in the doorway, and into the street that echoed with screams of despair.

In a routine formulated with Teutonic compassion, Anna and Ignacy Czeberowski were separated out from lower races and tagged as *Polish*. Grieving took place alongside a slop bucket on a train to a holding camp where Anna worked as a seamstress and waited for allocation to a concentration camp. Her skill and hard work kept them alive until Anna heard they were going to a special concentration camp for women called Ravensbrück. Their SS guards didn't provide any food or water on the train journey, which gave them a taste of what the future might hold. It set Anna and her son on a path to expectant death.

27

1944 Germany

Icy held his mother's hand and they were pushed into the medical theatre at Ravensbrück to stand before the SS doctors who were in conversation with a man who was obviously important from his uniform. A woman with a shaved head stood in the corner and the important man barked something at her in a strange language. The important man spoke to the woman with no hair for a long time and waved his finger in her face. She nodded when he pointed at his mother, Anna.

The woman with the shaved head talked to his mother and touched the blond hair that fell over her shoulders. They spoke in Polish and he couldn't hear much but she repeated the mysterious words *social or medical* over and over. Each time his mother shook her head to say no. Then the important man called one of the doctors who pulled his mother away. Anna told Icy not to move and the doctor and the woman with no hair walked with his mother to the end of the room and went behind a screen.

Everything was quiet after the loud voice of the important man. Icy could hear someone crying behind the screen, and hoped it was not his mother.

The voice of the woman with the shaved head became clear and all the others looked at the screen while the important man paced the floor. Icy heard *social or medical* again then, his mother and the woman with the shaved head came out from the screen. He could still hear another woman crying. His mother's face was whiter than he'd ever seen it. Her body shook as she walked across the room, which was strange because it was warm in here.

The important man said something to the woman with the shaved head who nodded but her body shook too. She spoke in Polish to his mother and said The Commandant ordered her to be clear about his generous offer. The woman said if Anna accepted his *social* offer, she kept her son and hair. Her assignment was for six months. His other option meant her head was shaved and the boy used immediately for their *medical* research scheme investigating leg wounds like those she saw behind the screen.

Anna spoke in Polish and accepted the offer and the other woman turned to the important man and said something to him in his own language. For the first time he smiled and spoke to the woman with the shaved head who told Icy to leave with her because, the SS doctors wanted to examine his mother for their records. The woman with the shaved head took his hand and led him to the door. When he looked back, he saw his mother unbutton her blouse. There was a red triangle on it that folded and reminded him of Dudel's game with paper animals. Icy trailed behind the woman with the shaved head who had a triangle on her blouse but it was different from his mother's and was yellow. Icy asked what it meant and she said *Jew* but he didn't understand and hurried to keep up.

*

28

The Caribbean - San Juan - Isla Grande Airport

Tuesday 14.00 - 22nd February 1966

Icy's driver was called Sexto and he was crying. Icy had fired him again and the driver was taking it bad.

'I told ya,' said Icy.

'He's crying,' said Henry.

'I just fired him,' said Icy.

'Why?'

Icy looked heavenward and held out his hands, 'they ain't a cloud up there to bring rain and this fuckbrain switches on the windshield wipers.'

'I did a mistake,' said Sexto.

'Shut up. Ya know what kinda sound wipers make on a dry screen. The kinda sound I can't stand that makes me crazy and wears out the rubber. Think of the money,' said Icy.

'I pay for new blades,' said Sexto.

'How ya gonna pay for setting my lousy teeth on edge? I still hear that rubber on the glass.'

Henry said, 'hire him back.'

'Listen fuckbrain,' Icy said, 'ya do that one more time I gonna have you taken up in the Beech and dropped in the sea like you was potatoes. Give me the keys and I drive. Sort out the cargo, then get lost.'

'OK Icy.' Sexto stopped crying and got out of the car.

Icy drove into town and it was noisy because he refused to shift higher than second gear and the engine raced. Nobody drove slower than Icy.

'I reverse faster than this.'

'Shut up. These Puerto Ricans drive like the streets are a racetrack.'

'Wake me when we get there,' Henry closed his eyes and listened to the giggles of the girl stretched out on the back seat reading a comic book.

'She a lazy mother like Sexto.'

'You teach her with comic books,' Henry said without opening his eyes.

'I buy her kids stuff with pictures.'

'Why not fire Sexto permanent?'

'No other driver cries like him and I'm sentimental. That's why I keep the bum.'

'You really got heart Icy.'

They double-parked and left the girl in the car. A police officer watched from across the street and waved...Icy waved back.

'A guy feels secure with reliable cops about.'

'You fixed to come with me to Tortola?'

'We got work to do there,' said Icy.

'Gunter ordered flowers to put on his graves tomorrow.'

'Buy them and enjoy how they smell.'

Henry hobbled into the flower shop and said, 'make me a bouquet with roses.'

'Hey, this guy a friend so make it cost,' Icy said, 'a discount is good for dead people.'

'I don't aim to be dead.'

'It's a principle with money.'

'Mix in some ferns,' Henry said.

'What's wrong with your foot?'

'Sea urchin spines.'

'Bad timing kid.'

'They hurt.'

The florist had orchids from El Yunque rain forest in the centre of Puerto Rico and mixed them with the roses. The orchids looked cold like Gunter.

'Sexto cries because he's poor, Icy.'

'It happens. My mother was poor and she cried,' said Icy.

'What about your old man?'

'My stepfather was a poor Jew.' Icy's hands went mad and Henry understood the shapes. He must've loved this stepfather.

'What'd he do?'

Icy said, 'he got sent to work on a project for Hitler with other clever Jews. They built rockets.'

'But you remember him?'

'Last time we spoke was in a place called Auschwitz. After he left, I figured he was alive until a guy in Israel told me he saw him in this factory. They tied his wrists behind and hung him on a hook for the other workers to see until his heart burst,' said Icy, 'he was disrespectful to a guard.'

'Could be a mistake,' said Henry.

'He's dead and that's another reason my mother cried,' said Icy.

Roses and orchids blended in a riot of colour tied together in a bouquet. Icy's girl thought they were for her and he didn't say different when they got in the car. She clutched them and her white teeth gleamed through the transparent wrapping.

'She thinks I bought them for her,' said Icy.

'She'll get over it.'

'Take a look at that smile. It's worth a bunch of flowers at cost,' Icy said and went to order the same again from the shop.

When he got back in the car Icy told the girl, 'this bunch is for him so keep your mitts off,' and then said it again in French.

'Mine are for a grave and yours for a girl. Different customers.'

'What a joke that dead people get flowers and can't see them,' said Icy.

'Gunter said the same thing.'

'Is that right?' said Icy.

'He made a chair.'

'I got chairs,' said Icy.

'Those vibrating chairs make me sick. His rocking chair doesn't need a motor.'

'You saw it?'

'Last I heard it was at Meath's house to deliver to the airport,' said Henry, 'Gunter said fly it to San Juan tomorrow and ship it same day to New York.'

'We take it for a souvenir.'

'Sure.'

Icy drove through the city and traffic built-up behind them.

'This is a big hit,' said Henry.

'After it's done ya vanish, kid.'

'I'm your top boy Icy. Mixed Palestinian and British blood like me has style.'

'Ya head is stupid with broads.'

'Women take my mind off getting killed.'

'Ya got nerve and balls. Do tomorrow's job and beat it.'

'Yeah.'

'Forget everything but the hit.'

'Sharks almost got us on Sunday,' said Henry, 'me and Jayce went diving.'

'Still a Beirut wild man,' said Icy and his hands went mad again, 'two fucking years planning and ya play around with sharks.'

'Jayce got in trouble on the reef and I pulled him out.'

'He owes ya.'

'He's been sweet eyeballed by Gunter,' said Henry, 'but there's something else about him smells funny.'

'Tell me what smells.'

'I smell Jayce is foreign competition,' said Henry.

'Ya got a nose for competition.'

'Icy, whatever happens, Italia's pregnant.'

'I'll take care of her kid,' he needed Henry's mind on the hit but Icy never broke his word.

In the car, the girl wrapped her arms around the bouquet and smiled through the blooms.

'Ten bucks of flowers and she's happy.'

'We waste our final guy tomorrow.'

'And after it's over there's a final offer from me.'

'What sort of offer?' said Henry.

'I ain't figured it out yet.'

'The countdown's started in my head. I need to know the time to move on Gunter.'

'After the bridge opens is good. Use The Queen for cover.'

'It'll go wrong If Gunter runs early to his birthday party.'

'He won't do that.'

Icy made the shape of an aeroplane with his hands and Henry did the same.

'What sort of Jew are you Icy?'

'A Catholic one from Poland.'

'Pretty unusual I make hits for Israel arranged by a Christian boss.'

'You a half Palestinian defector...both of us made sacrifices.'

'We need that white dame's house for position. That's a sacrifice,' said Henry.

'Ya got that covered. Right now we work the supermarket and buy The Queen some cookies to celebrate her big day.'

'There's bigger things to celebrate when we both walk away.'

*

29

The Caribbean - San Juan

Tuesday 14.30 - 22nd February 1966

Icy claimed he got his education renting out skates at an ice rink and the name stuck. But Icy's kindergartens were in the Warsaw ghetto and Nazi concentration camps. Later schooling came on the streets of Beirut. Nobody asked him his proper name and his cover was absolute. Icy preferred a crowded environment to stay invisible and liked Old San Juan for that reason. They crossed the causeway to the narrow streets of the old city and walked along the blue cobbles of Morcado Street.

'These houses are painted orange and green.'

'I wanted that you peek at this place. While you were in the sky, I'm on the streets of the old city.'

Icy led them to the fountain in the centre of Quinto Centenario Square. Sunlight flashed through the columns of spray and dappled the ground. They sat on the side of the fountain.

'Drop your hand in the water kid and the water don't recognise it. Take your hand out and it don't leave a hole behind. Your hand don't exist for the water. Me and you won't exist after tomorrow.'

'You're losing me Icy.'

'We gonna have wet hands tomorrow but nobody remembers us when it's done and the water settles.'

'We're short of time.'

At the supermarket in San Juan, they threw food in a trolley.

'Haiti is a cheap place for girls,' said Icy, 'I paid fifty bucks for mine.'

'They cost me a dollar there.'

'Not the hookers. This one is permanent and I paid her folks. She fools about in those chairs and cooks.'

'Seems you just talk about women.'

Icy laughed, 'when I was a little boy there was this place we lived where there was nothing but screwing. It made me care less about sex. Stay long enough in the supermarket with food and pretty soon you ain't hungry.'

They stood at the meat counter and the Puerto Rican butcher came over.

'A dozen pork chops,' said Henry.

'You gentiles eat dirty meat,' said Icy.

'Tastes good.'

'It ain't kosher.'

'You're not a Jew.'

'I play orthodox and gotta stick to that part.'

The manager of the supermarket brought a carton of chocolate milk for Icy. He allowed them to eat and drink what they wanted in the store because they spent so much. Icy took a swig.

'Try some,' he held out the carton.

'Your veins must be clogged.'

'I don't drink or smoke,' said Icy.

'Two quarts of chocolate milk a day is worse than booze and you keep skinny.'

'Running you as a hitter keeps me skinny.'

They used a special checkout girl because she was fast. Icy threw items out to her and Henry packed bags.

'Something about this bugs me,' said Icy, 'I gotta figure how to put it together. Gunter is our man all right but that ain't enough to solve the puzzle.'

'That's your problem.'

'It's gotta be worked out before I give the go-ahead to kill him.'

'He uses an American passport.'

'Any jerk can buy a passport. Remind me about his tastes.'

'He does wood. At the back of his dress shop he built a rocking chair and carves puppets that hang on the wall like an audience.'

'Puppets catch my interest.'

'You'd notice them.'

'How big are they?'

'So big,' Henry measured in the air, 'wooden puppets in strange clothes circle the place. They've got heads made of wood and human faces.'

'You want keep a secret, give it to someone with a wooden head.'

The hands of the checkout girl were a blur on her cash register. For a second she looked up and Henry smiled. The operation froze before Icy's eyes and he moved into Henry's space before she could return the usual loving glance.

'What more have you got on our man?'

'Like I mentioned, I flew his boyfriend into St Thomas to catch a jet to New York. He was beat up pretty bad and wanted to talk and who knows, maybe he will one day. It was his way to settle things but he's got more secrets. He didn't blab the real stuff but said enough.'

'Enough?'

'Karl doesn't know who I am so his mouth is loose and I pick up that Gunter is ready to move out tomorrow. Another thing, Gunter got burned at the top of his left arm. On the inside is a patch of skin that's been treated with acid.'

'Show me where.'

'About here.'

'Is that right?'

'Yeah,' said Henry, 'and I heard The Doctor tell Jayce about it.'

'Those Aryans liked their blood group tattooed there so they never got transfused with blood from lower races. All before your time, kid.'

'He's no pushover Icy.'

'The guy is known to me and those mothers in Israel set me up to make a positive ID. The Mossad bastards knew I saw him before.'

'Talk through the set up.'

'We definitely found our man and I gotta hunch where he hid the stuff Tel Aviv wants so bad. Fly me to Tortola and we split at the airport. My belief is competitors want the same stuff and will break cover if they figure Gunter is moving out...we gotta be first. Let's talk through our plan on the flight.'

'You got a number that looks like a blood group tattooed on your arm, Icy.'

'A symbol kid...B6174 is the number from a crowd I hung out with.'

'You ever see the others?'

'They moved on.'

*

In late afternoon, Henry lifted off the runway at Isla Grande downtown airport. There was a hotel on the right of his take-off path but he held the plane down after he raised the gear and went past the second story at eye level.

'Would ya look at that dame in the bedroom? Hey slow up and go round again.'

'She was too old for you.'

'Goddamn.'

'Why burn gas to look, Icy?'

'Because looking's what I like best.'

They passed San Juan International airport and left the coast for the familiar trip home. Vieques Island and Culebra drifted past to the right on their last ride to Tortola.

'Deliver those flowers to Gunter,' said Icy, 'and they guarantee he'll stay for the celebrations tomorrow.'

'You understand him.'

'Like he was an old friend. First thing tomorrow he'll take them up the mountain to the graves. Get in position behind him.'

Icy told him how to keep Gunter locked on the mountainside.

'The only way to the shack is through the courtyard of the big house,' said Henry.

'Follow him and hide with the white dame. Gunter's stuck on the mountain till the party's over and she'll make the shindig last for you. Do your thing and we get together in the mangroves.'

'You're certain he's the right guy?'

'It's him for sure and he's gonna run to his buddy in New York to eat birthday cake if we don't stop him.'

'Hits are dirty most times,' said Henry, 'and Gunter is tricky.'

'Make this one clean.'

'After the hit, we fly to San Juan and split. I stashed an escape bag with some clothes in the hold of the Beech.'

'Good. And then I gotta be tricky with our boys in Tel Aviv and rig it so the powers think you were killed doing the job. Mossad don't let hitters retire.'

*

30

1960 Beirut - Icy

When his mother died Icy became an Israeli orphan. The education system recognised his gift of languages and the intelligence services identified other talents. With his Teutonic looks, Icy would never be taken as Jewish but he knew about surviving in concentration camps. His Israeli boss got him work in a carpet emporium on Beirut's seafront. He slept on the floor with the protection of a knife against the beggars outside. Fluent languages got Icy promotion at the carpet shop and he rented a small apartment in the Basta quarter close to a cemetery. Israeli intelligence realised he was invisible but his contribution was little more than dead letter drops with information about political visitors to the shop on the Beirut seafront. All his instructions came from an unseen controller called Michael.

Whenever Icy felt lonely, he talked to Dudel and Anna and told them about the carpets he sold. Once he was ordered to kill a Syrian who was the last customer of the day and hid the corpse in a roll of carpet until he could ease it into the sea at the back of the shop. Icy distracted the beggars with food pushed outside the front door. He knew how starvation centred the mob and while they scavenged, he dragged the body into the sea. It was his first murder and he decided in future to pay others with more appetite for death's work.

Icy spoke to Dudel, 'this wasn't the way you wanted for me but it got tough after you were sent away. That time in the cell was a minute, but mother and I never forgot the last time the three of us were together. I wanted to say things but you saw my fingers and know what they meant because you taught me how to talk with them.'

'And another thing mother,' he said to Anna, 'there isn't a day I don't look at your picture. Please know I'm a good son but this is what I do until we meet up again...it'll be soon. Stay patient.'

One day, Michael called him by phone and said, 'turn your heart to steel and obey orders. Turn your heart to God after.'

'What God have you in mind? I asked God questions before and there was no one home.'

Michael said, 'do what Israel orders and when this work is over go back to your army career.' Icy wondered about the next steps of his secret existence.

Icy became general manager of the carpet shop and organised his own work schedule. On the last Friday of August he was instructed to walk down the seafront and meet Michael in person. Until then Michael was an invisible voice. Michael sidled alongside Icy on the Corniche. They went to the bar of an old French hotel overlooking the sea and Michael said this was a safe place to meet but didn't explain why. He said that Michael, meant *Messenger of God* in Hebrew and that was useful because it was a common name in other languages. It was not his real name but if ever Icy was tortured, he could disclose it.

'Ten guys beat the shit out of me for information and all I tell them is Michael means *Messenger of God*. My belief is they keep on beating.'

'It gives them something to think about,' said Michael.

'It won't make them stop,' said Icy.

'They never stop,' said Michael, 'you know that.'

Michael was fat in a way that made his face difficult to remember but it was hard to forget what he said. He told Icy about the Palestinian fighters who used a particular cemetery in Beirut if an associate was killed, which was one of the few times you saw them in a bunch. He said it was called the Bashoura Cemetery, near to Icy's apartment and he wanted him to hang out there because there was a young buck who needed attention. Icy asked if he wanted him killed but he said just the opposite, they wanted to make him one of their own. Big shots in Israel heard Icy had street credibility and could turn the kid. They'd let him know what direction to turn.

'Decide the lure,' said Michael.

'Women or money usually work.'

'This kid is different.'

'What are my limits?'

'Whatever it takes,' said Michael, 'he likes aeroplanes. But there's something he likes more.'

Icy asked was he certain this kid would show up at the cemetery and Michael said he went there every day to watch funerals and throw rocks at the mourners and was mostly alone. Michael told Icy to use his instinct and get him in the fold. Once he was hooked, they wanted Icy to be his controller. Michael said they knew the kid was a serial killer with an appetite for murder, which was a bonus. Another bonus was his British father and the passport that went with it. Michael said the kid's father was a diplomat, who'd married a Palestinian woman.

Icy wondered why the kid was so wild with respectable parents. Michael said his mother got killed when he was young and then he ran about with the Palestinian bucks. Icy said he could understand. The embassy paid for him at a private school. He was educated but liked the extreme side of life better, and his father wasn't interested. Michael knew what might hook the kid and turn him to their thinking and he explained about the women.

'Palestinian mothers worship their sons,' said Icy.

'His mother got killed and he worshipped her,' said Michael.

'That leaves his old man.'

'He's found a Persian bed mate with no taste for a mongrel stepson who runs with Beirut gunmen. It would do papa a favour if the kid ended up dead like his mother.'

'We need to turn the old man if he acts as a block,' said Icy.

'Use your imagination,' said Michael.

Michael put some money on the table and a note with the kid's name on it. The bar was furnished in wood stained nicotine brown from cigarette smoke. Late sunlight caught the smoke from a man at the bar who spoke English to the barman and added a few words in French. As Michael left he whispered to the barman and went out. The barman came over and asked in Arabic if he wanted anything and Icy said he was leaving now. Three languages spoken in as many minutes like it was normal. Michael told him the kid spoke them all and he wondered which to use when they met. English seemed a good idea and this was a good place to bring him, where people used three languages. Show him the place was safe.

But that was down the line so he picked up the money and went to pay. The barman wanted to chat and show off the cameras he stored behind the bar. The barman's wife came in and they talked a while. Icy gave her some money and said he'd come back soon with work for her. Through a window, Icy saw the lights on a jet climbing out over the bay and his fingers worked at the note in his hand to make a shape because it seemed a good sign. The barman followed him out and asked in Arabic if everything was satisfactory for a friend of Michael. Icy told the barman to keep his cameras ready at short notice for a visit by a special guest who needed the full treatment from his wife. The jet was almost out of sight heading towards Europe and he flagged a taxi to go home and think about meeting this crazy kid at the Bashoura cemetery.

*

31

1960 Beirut - Henry

Henry thought the small funeral at the Bashoura cemetery was not worth throwing rocks at but there was this guy with blond hair and funny hands who came over and talked to him. He told the guy there was plenty of action around here these days with things getting rough in the city and people killed a lot. The cemetery overlooked the airport flight path and Henry liked to watch the aircraft land and take-off between throwing rocks at the mourners. Once in a while, professional mourners were hired to wail for the dead and it was funny how they could suddenly curse when a stone hit them flush.

'You got a good eye for throwing rocks. Hey, my name is Icy...how come you never hit the corpse?'

'There's no fun with that. There's more juice to hit the live ones and make them screech. My name is Henry.'

'Is this what you do for fun? It's kinda lonely out here by the cemetery.'

'It's hard to make friends in the city,' said Henry.

'That's strange for a young guy.'

'Not strange for a mixed-blood, Palestinian fighter.'

'But the cemetery is a lonely place,' said Icy.

'With a great view of the planes coming in to land.'

'I guess you like planes?'

'More than anything.'

'OK,' said Icy.

Icy made the shape of an aeroplane with his hands and asked Henry what he would give to fly one of those. Henry said just about anything but there was no way to do it. Icy asked why his father couldn't pay for him to learn to fly and Henry said because he'd taken up with a Persian woman and wanted to go to Iran when he retired and got rid of his son. The old man was mean and there was nobody else. His father was British and worked at the embassy and his Palestinian mother was dead, but Icy already knew that.

'Listen. Say I take a shine to a Palestine boy with potential. Good looks and other shit. Someone who knows how to keep his mouth shut about high value transactions. In my business those qualities pay off.'

'What business?'

'Carpets,' said Icy, 'and there might be something we can work on with the flying stuff.'

Icy took Henry to Michael's bar near the sea with the dark wood inside. It was quiet and elegant. A man came in, and put on a white jacket and said something in Arabic and went behind the bar to serve drinks but he talked to other drinkers in different languages. Then, a woman came in and sat at the bar. She was the most beautiful thing ever and Icy asked if he wanted to meet her because that was possible. Henry said yes and Icy called her over and left them together while he got drinks and that was the start because she moved fast. She said she did modelling and they used this place because it was an authentic French hotel. There was a room upstairs, where she rested between photographic shoots and Henry might like to see it. Icy sat at the same table when Henry came back thirty minutes later.

'Don't try blackmail again, your camera guy was noisy,' said Henry.

'He don't make any noise. How did you know?'

'Me and her met before,' said Henry.

'Never trust a beautiful woman.'

'Not with me,' said Henry.

Icy said how about if he made Henry a business proposal where he learned to fly and eventually got a job away from this place. Henry said what about the money and the old man but Icy said he could fix both things if he would act as a representative of his carpet business. They needed people who spoke different languages.

'The old man won't be easy to swing. He gets prim when it isn't his idea.'

'Prim can be useful. I got ways of using prim,' said Icy.

'You won't get anything to shift him,' said Henry.

'No harm in trying. Give me a month.'

Three weeks later, Henry's father mentioned about learning to fly and left it hanging. He'd found a useful contact and Henry knew who it was. Icy never came to their house but met Henry's father at the same bar in the French hotel and negotiated an agreement to sponsor his son. All fully confidential and that suited both of them. Once, when Henry returned to the bar by himself the barman's wife came and sat with him for a while. She said his father came here a few times with Icy and she had pictures of him somewhere. Please send her regards to him.

'I'll pass them on,' said Henry.

'Palestinian and British blood mix well in you,' she said.

'Icy says nobody knows which side I'm on.'

'Icy misses nothing and he collects photographs,' she said with an innocent expression.

Back home, Henry told his father about the woman in the hotel who sent her regards and when he described her, it was as if he'd been shot. His father said not to mention this to anyone in Beirut in case his fiancé heard. When Henry told his father about going to America to learn to fly, he didn't act surprised and said it was probably for the best and would keep him away from the Palestinian fighters. Henry said flight schools in the sunshine states meant he would qualify quickly because the weather was good for training and then he'd find a job. Henry's father was relieved at this news and said he was going to marry his Persian girlfriend and go and live in the mountains near Shiraz. There was no other family so a new career and a move away from Beirut seemed a good idea for his son. Henry said things had worked out and he wanted to leave quickly and that seemed OK with his father. They were not close.

Icy came to see his father and things happened fast at the embassy and his British passport was all in order to travel with an American visa. Icy said it was useful having a British father who was an embassy official. It was funny but at the end, his father seemed frightened when Icy came to pick him up and the front door was shut by the time he got in the car for the airport. Henry said the old man seemed scared but Icy said some people get afraid when they see a picture of themselves and maybe he was superstitious. He asked what he meant about a picture but Icy didn't answer and said he would make sure the old man was looked after when he left and not to worry. Just learn to fly. Icy told him there was other training to do but Henry was used to handling guns so it was more secret procedures and stuff like that.

Henry said, 'if you have pictures give them all to the old man. You've got me now and pictures would kill him. Let him go to Shiraz with his new woman and a pension. I won't see him again. Do me this favour.'

'There's two sets of pictures, kid. He has one set and this is the second,' Icy pulled an envelope from his bag and gave it to Henry, 'now you got the copies. Don't look at them.'

'Stop so I can burn them,' said Henry.

The drive to the airport took them near a Palestinian refugee camp and Icy said to keep his head down until they got on the airport road where there were no fighters. Their driver stopped next to a drain and Henry held the pictures face down and burned each one and dropped the debris in the sewer.

'At least I can remember him like he was, with my mother.'

'Clean break kid. That woman in the pictures was very persuasive,' said Icy.

'She tried to persuade me to run off with her and ditch that barman husband. Not so persuasive,' said Henry.

'That bitch bit my hand after all the dough she had for pictures. What a bitch.'

'You can trust me with women Icy.'

'I can't trust women with you.'

'Leave them to me.'

It was quick at the airport and Icy ran through Henry's schedule. His flight was on Pan Am to New York. Icy gave him a bunch of dollars to see him through to flight school. They stared ahead at the mountains of Lebanon, and Icy whispered orders switching languages to make his point and at the end, there was no doubt in either mind that Henry was a bought man. Icy paid and owned him and when they shook hands at the departure gate, it confirmed their arrangement for Henry's loan. The number of murders was agreed before Henry got free of his debt. The burned pictures of Henry's father unofficially sealed their trust as partners. But what really sealed their contract were the risks Icy promised. Death was the highest possible stake for an addicted killer like Henry and he wanted to gamble with the best.

*

32

1947 New York

Martha Gold wrote a confidential memo to two private mailboxes in New York – it was unsigned.

Hjalmar Schacht was detained as a conspirator in the 1944 bomb plot to assassinate Hitler. He was sent to Ravensbrück, Flossenberg and Dachau concentration camps. In 1945, Schacht was arrested and charged with war crimes by American liberators. He stood trial at Nuremberg in 1946. At that trial, he requested a plea bargain to save his skin but the offer was refused by Justice Jackson of the United States. The crimes of which he stood accused carried the death penalty. Schacht was acquitted and released on 1st October 1946.

I would be pleased to brief you on the circumstances at your earliest convenience and suggest we meet at the usual venue.

Yours etc.

*

The suite in The Algonquin Hotel was unchanged and the men wore similar clothes. Martha wore an expensive jacket and skirt. Her hair was perfect but she was too well dressed for an FBI agent's salary. The men paid Martha Gold to talk and obtained value by listening.

Martha shuffled her papers and said, 'this information is still classified but we'll go back to where I came in six years ago.' The men understood.

'In 1941 a yacht vanished in The Caribbean. On it were funds due to your corporations,' she had the men's attention now. 'There was a planned explosion on the boat designed to kill all four people on board. Two of them were in a cabin under the main deck when the incendiary device exploded and they escaped the burning yacht in a dinghy. They saw the yacht sink and the US Navy picked them up drifting in The Puerto Rico Trench area. These men were security agents for your corporations. If the courier employed by Germany for this transaction is located, they can identify him. Only the courier could have set up the explosion and we guess he stole the genuine funds. No one knows how.'

The thin man in black said, 'we paid you for this. Is there extra worth listening to?'

'You decide,' said Martha, 'your cheque isn't cashed.'

The other man said, 'forget that...we want to know what happened.'

The thin man said, 'fuck what happened if we get the money.'

'Money won't matter if we don't get the receipts.'

Martha raised her hands to keep the peace. Rich men hate being screwed.

She said, 'decide if I cash it,' and put their cheque on a coffee table, 'or you tear it up.'

The thin man said, 'go on.'

Martha said, 'this is new stuff nobody but us can know about or where it got raised. Where we start is with Hjalmar Schacht - Hitler's financier and an old friend of you guys,' and Martha watched them squirm. 'At the Nuremberg War Crimes Tribunal, people got tried for their lives and pulled off deals. Schacht was better than the rest. We start with his interrogation. Forget the affidavit shit written down in legal papers.'

Martha took a sip of water, 'there are three big players at his interrogation. America, Britain and Russia – the French passed on the meeting. Whatever Schacht says Russia will demand the death penalty. If you were betting men, he was dead. We have three colonels present from those countries and the interrogation is in English because they all speak English except the Russian so he has an interpreter. Plus me as an FBI observer.'

Martha moved about, 'Schacht is cute and stalls for an hour until the Russian interpreter goes out to take a leak then he whispers fast to the Brit and Yank in English and the Russian colonel looks dumb. Schacht says he plans to give testimony about a commercial transaction in 1941, carried out on British territory to pay money to two American corporations. Amongst other ways, these funds were collected from Hitler's Jewish confiscation programme and the US corporations had full knowledge of their source. He won't give this testimony if they cut him a deal at the tribunal. Suddenly the Brit and the Yank are beat with high voltage. Obviously neither knew this stuff and the Russian is staring at his cigarette.'

Now the captains of industry were listening hard, 'the British and American guys talk in a hurry but the Russian interpreter comes back and it goes quiet. I guess the American colonel figures it's worth flying a kite and looks at the Brit. He says in his opinion the charges Herr Schacht face are questionable and proposes a plea bargain arrangement. The British guy nods and I wait for an explosion when the interpreter gives this to the Russian colonel.'

Martha milked the silence, 'they look at the Russian and he stays calm. Remember, this guy tells Soviet judges what to do. Make no mistake he's NKVD and calls the shots. He speaks to his interpreter and we all wait for the shit to hit but the interpreter looks as if he doesn't understand. The Russian colonel presses his arm to remind him who's who and the interpreter says the colonel agrees with this proposal and will do what he can with his people on behalf of Herr Schacht.'

The industrialists exchanged glances, 'it's unreal in there,' said Martha, 'since when do Russians agree clemency for a high ranking Nazi. It looks like they all want to get out of the room. The guards take Schacht out first and the others stay in their chairs. Next up are the American and British boys and they shake hands with the Russian. He stays sat down with me behind him. As the two colonels get to the door the Yank shouts back, "what's your name lady?" and I say "Martha". They say, "so long Martha," and go out so there's just me, the Russian and his interpreter.'

Martha waited a couple of beats, 'his interpreter goes out and there's me and the Russian colonel left alone. He says, "so long Martha," and I figure he's mimicking and say, "so long," back. "No," he says, "it's so long Yegor...my name is Yegor Akulov." He spoke good English.' Martha gathered her thoughts, 'Akulov stays cool as you like and goes on, "Martha, I know what happened to those funds Herr Schacht can testify about," and clams up. You want my opinion gents. Schacht and Akulov know everything you want between them. You got channels to Schacht I guess and maybe Akulov strolls across your path in the future. That's my pitch for the cheque,' the thin man pushed it across to her.

Martha tucked the cheque in her purse and said, 'here's a bonus, on the house. I stick around Nuremberg as an FBI observer but try to get close to Akulov. I figure his day of glory is to come. Time goes by and the Brits and Yanks press the American prosecutor, Justice Jackson for a plea bargain with Schacht. He tells them to fuck off and says Schacht is guilty as shit like the rest of the Nazi pack. People get hot under the collar. Schacht's testimony is political dynamite and can blow Nuremberg sky high.'

'Get to the point,' said the thin man.

'The point is if Schacht gives this *precise* testimony there's a chance those American corporations he names get indicted for war crimes. Or their head guys?' For the first time Martha saw their arrogance waiver. 'Schacht testified on April thirtieth,' and she thought the man in the hat would have a heart attack.

Martha said, 'relax; you and your outfits are in the clear. That's the bonus.'

The thin man's voice cracked when he spoke, 'how do you know for certain?'

'The Brits and Yanks get to work on their judges and bring the French onboard but if the Russians dig in, Schacht probably hangs like his buddies. Now, my guess is Akulov tells the Russian judge to look angry and dissent, but to ride along with the others if it goes to the wire. When Herr Schacht gives his testimony, would you believe he says nothing about the transaction in 1941. Then a miracle happens and they find him not guilty on both counts he's charged with and he walks. Yes sir, Hitler's Minister of the Economy goes free. Nobody believes it until it happens and it definitely happened. One day you guys might bump into Colonel Akulov and ask about your dough, but I figure he saved your bacon...and me being a Jew thinks that's funny.'

33

The Caribbean - Tortola

Tuesday 16.00 - 22nd February 1966

Meath stared across the runway to the cay in Trellis Bay. He spoke in Spanish with his back to Gelson.

'Nuestras madres Puerto Rico nos dio a los españoles a hablar con él allá Gelson,'...*our Puerto Rican mothers gave us the Spanish to talk to him over there Gelson.*

'He spoke Spanish perfect Meath.'

'Things went wrong in '41 but my brain says it's him.'

'He never saw our faces.'

'It's him.'

'I remember his mush,' said Gelson.

'You electrocuted the wrong guy last time.'

'It was you who fingered him Meath, and swore it was the right guy.'

'The doc put it down as a heart attack. We got lucky with those burn marks.'

'Shouldn't have happened with high voltage and low current. You know how good I am with the prod to make them squeal.'

'This one is strong. Twenty-five years to get even and find how he pulled the con,' said Meath.

'He'll talk with my electric prod,' said Gelson.

'Other parties might've tip toed in to look for our stuff.'

'You figured out who's who?' Gunter's car pulled up outside the bar.

'I got an idea.'

Meath set a can of beer on the bar for Gunter.

'Catching up with things,' said Meath pointing at Gelson's magazine.

'Sure, we need news. This place is dead,' said Gunter. He took a swig from his beer and held out his hand to Gelson, 'welcome to paradise.'

Gelson put his drink on the counter and shook hands. Gunter held Gelson's right hand for a while until he pulled away to pick up his coke bottle.

'See you all later,' Gunter slammed his beer on the counter and left.

'He's in a hurry,' Meath said when Gunter drove off.

'That's him,' Gelson was excited and his bottle slipped and broke on the floor, 'real sorry Meath.'

'No problem,' said Meath and kicked the glass into a pile.

'Now I saw him we can start. Let's talk later when things are finished.'

'Get it done Gelson. No hitches.'

'Right on.'

Gelson checked the contents of his bag at Meath's bar. The battery and leads were there to coax Gunter's story with electricity. Gelson flagged a taxi and settled into the air conditioning of Gassy's vehicle.

'Where to?' said Gassy.

'Someplace in town.'

'A bar OK?'

'OK,' said Gelson, 'make it quick.'

'About twenty minutes,' said Gassy.

'OK.'

*

34

1942 Russia

Hitler's invasion of Russia consumed German soldiers with an insatiable appetite. After his rendezvous on the Caribbean cay, Gunter was sent to the eastern front where neither side expected or received mercy from the other. Things were desperate for Russia and their soldiers fought hard to slow down the German advance. German commanders usually executed Russians captured at the front, but some non-Russians were spared. Gunter's field commander scanned his execution warrant and noticed two identical surnames. They weren't Russian names and he called his orderly to check them out.

The orderly returned and said the men were Polish brothers pressed into service by the Russians. They offered to fight for Germany if their lives were spared and had firsthand knowledge of Russian troop locations. The commander asked if they spoke German and the orderly said no, they were questioned by an SS soldier who spoke Polish. He asked to see the soldier and the orderly brought in Gunter.

The field commander told Gunter he wanted to use the Polish brothers on a reconnaissance operation to Russian lines but needed a German volunteer to lead them. Gunter agreed but asked for support from a brother SS soldier who also spoke Polish. The request for Karl was granted. Their mission was to identify Russian artillery locations using the Polish brothers as guides. Capture meant certain death. The German commander needed location coordinates for Russian artillery, fast. Gunter was given seventy-two hours for the mission and would be presumed dead after that deadline. Wearing SS uniforms, the four men left in the early hours of the next morning.

In no man's land, Karl said, 'the Russians fire plenty of shells but don't hit much.'

'Head for those artillery flashes and our Poles will run at the guns if we order them. Shot or captured, we march with dead men,' Gunter said.

'They're crazy.'

'If it gets bad, use them to draw fire off us,' said Gunter.

They walked to the front steered by gun flashes. The brothers insisted the Russian lines were a long way ahead.

When the barrage stopped, the silence came alive with noises and they heard talking. It was difficult to locate the voices and they pressed on but were near Russian troops.

'Close means near enough for intelligence,' Gunter spoke in Polish to the brothers, 'but don't get captured or we rub shoulders in a grave.' He pulled the brothers and Karl into a shell hole.

'I think they took us too far,' said Karl.

'At daylight we crawl out,' Gunter said and edged to the rim of the hole as darkness thinned into light.

'We could turn back now,' said Karl.

'There's no chance of that.'

In the dim light, they were surrounded by shimmering bayonets. Gunter knew this illusion came from rancid pig fat that Siberian troops smeared on the steel to guarantee infection when they stabbed Germans. The Siberians had flat, impassive faces and there were hundreds of them because Gunter's quartet was hunkered down behind Russian lines. They laid down their weapons and walked to the nearest bayonets.

*

The Red Army employed officers of the NKVD secret police to spread terror and motivate front line troops. NKVD men sat behind their army's front line and any Russian soldier who turned away from the enemy was shot. Soldiers didn't retreat. Still further away from the front line was the intelligence arm of the NKVD that questioned captured Germans. The four captives were taken there for interrogation and execution at the office of Yegor Akulov. Battlefield intelligence needed quick answers and death inevitably followed questioning. Occasionally, Akulov used another way on those he identified as future assets.

Colonel Yegor Akulov was a protégé of Lavrenti Pavlovitch Beria - the head of the NKVD who'd educated him in exceptional psychological methods for turning selected prisoners into agents of the state. Identifying promising Russian spies was left to Akulov's sergeant who also carried out executions. Akulov's sergeant was trained in the medical skills required for their sophisticated form of psychological coercion.

Akulov used a shell-damaged police station for his interrogations. Afterwards, prisoners were executed with their mouths stuffed with sawdust and wrists tied with wire. When Gunter arrived, Akulov's sergeant had shot thirty Germans in the hour before, and stepped out for a smoke. The sergeant was intrigued by the capture of such a small group of prisoners and told his men not to beat them until Akulov was informed.

Akulov lay awake and bored during the artillery bombardment and was pleased to visit the four prisoners with his sergeant for a breakfast interrogation. The sergeant explained they'd captured two genuine Germans SS soldiers and two Polish soldiers dressed in SS uniforms. Akulov noticed that the two German men exchange glances and remarked on this bond. His sergeant joked that homosexual relationships were illegal in Germany and especially in the SS. It gave Akulov an idea - Beria's psychological technique for imposing total authority was simple. Crush a strong personality into a vacuum of fear and tip an unthinkable threat into the void to make them compliant forever. The Polish men were condemned as toys in this exercise. Akulov told his sergeant to prepare things now because if this was a reconnaissance party, they'd be expected back before long.

Next door to the execution cell, an interrogation room was set up for Akuolv's specialism. It was bare apart from a wooden chair bolted to the floor. Within fifteen minutes, one Polish prisoner was prepared and strapped in it with his head immobilised by a metal restraint. On either side of the restraint were leather blinkers so the prisoner could only look straight ahead. The sergeant circled the room holding a small dish and occasionally stopped behind the man and tapped it with a metal spatula. Yegor Akulov came in and an interpreter followed with Gunter whose wrists were tied with wire and his mouth stuffed with sawdust ready for execution. Akulov took Gunter behind the Polish captive.

    The interpreter said, 'our sergeant's skill is impressive and the colonel wants you to consider your position after you see him in action. The colonel does not speak German so I will translate.'

The sergeant had removed an area the size of a saucer from the back of the prisoner's skull with a brace and bit and exposed his brain. Akulov's interpreter explained to Gunter that a human brain has no nerve endings and this Polish traitor would not feel pain during the demonstration. Depending on the sergeant's skill, the traitor would lose control over his body functions as his brain was spooned out in small pieces and deposited in the dish. The cleverness lay in preventing bleeding and many subjects, though vegetative, stayed alive for two days or more. Observe.

Gunter faced the prisoner while the sergeant spooned brain tissue from the Polish man's head into the dish. The prisoner was silent and after twenty minutes, the sergeant showed Gunter the contents of the dish.

The interpreter said, 'your Polish traitor will now give you a compelling performance. I saw it many times.'

The prisoner went blind and lost control of his bowels. Akulov nodded approval and he and his interpreter went out and left Gunter and the sergeant together. The prisoner wept and pleaded until his speech went and then the sergeant took Gunter to a cell next door. There was a piece of sackcloth pulled across one wall. They listened to the cries of the Polish man until he coughed into silence. Afterwards, they heard sounds of more unseen activities.

After a few minutes, Akulov came in and his interpreter said to Gunter, 'the colonel asks if you enjoyed the artistry of our sergeant? He has a proposal. Nod or shake your head in reply when you observe our second presentation. The sergeant will leave us to prepare.'

The interpreter said, 'the colonel wants a decision but makes time for a second performance.' Akulov pulled away the cloth on the wall away to uncover a hole looking into the interrogation room. The chair and head restraint were locked in the same position and the sergeant stood behind the chair holding a brace and bit. The chair was side on so the prisoner couldn't see his observers because of the leather blinkers. Akulov held Gunter's arm and moved him to get a clear view of the prisoner. Karl's head was restrained by steel and he could see nothing or hear the cry from Gunter who was choked into silence by sawdust. But Akulov felt Gunter's arm tremble and knew he had his man.

Akulov dropped the curtain and the interpreter told Gunter the colonel was ready to listen but wanted to explain his proposal in detail. Depending on the reply, Gunter and his friend would be released back to their lines. If Gunter did not agree then work would begin on his friend and he would be obliged to watch another demonstration of Russian skill. Akulov spoke, allowing time between sentences for his interpreter to translate and Gunter to think.

'SS filth, you have an option but remember; I need more than betraying fellow Germans.' The colonel talked about German army positions he required and about another set of Russian gun locations for Gunter to hand to his commanding officer. He paused for the message to register and went on, 'these are important but your SS lover promised us more to avoid the bullet. He said you possessed secrets of great value and property worth much when the war is over. He begged for his life but had not the gift of those secrets...they were yours alone. You've seen the show and must convince me about your valuable secrets or the reprise starts with your lover. Reprise means you see it done again. Tell me your secret story to keep you both alive. Confess or watch your friend loose his brain and after, we put a bullet through your own head.'

Akulov held out his hands in question. Gunter nodded and the guard cut the wire binding him and waited while he vomited sawdust. The interpreter offered him water and when he could speak told him in German that they were ready to listen. Gunter spoke about his life and the SS for the next hour while the colonel made notes. He told Akulov everything he knew and bargained for Karl with his private story of the bonds and diamonds.

Akulov's interpreter gave him co-ordinates of Russian artillery positions for his field commander and wrote down the location of German forces that Gunter provided.

'Your German bombardment will start when they have these co-ordinates. That will satisfy one element of success in our venture,' and explained Gunter would be escorted halfway to the German lines and left to make his own way to base. As a precaution, Karl remained with them here until the German shelling began, and then returned by the same route with the papers of the dead Polish brothers, heroically killed in action. Speed was needed for this sort of intelligence.

'I recommend you keep clear of your command headquarters when the Russians answer back with their shells. Our gunners are accurate.'

Colonel Akulov wanted to make future contact using a special copy of *Mein Kampf* and planned to send reminders. The interpreter showed Gunter how to employ Hitler's literary masterpiece for one-off communications. It was simple and had no time limit. A few hours later Karl knew how to contact Akulov using the same method.

Outside the ruined police station, the Siberians waited to guide them through the Russian front lines. When they were ready to leave, Akulov's interpreter reminded Gunter they would always know where he was in years to come. Loyalty was cemented into Gunter's ruined psyche.

The interpreter smirked and said to Gunter in German, 'it is strange that only I know what was said between the three of us and so we must all stay in touch.' Then Akulov led Gunter away and they were alone.

They walked through the impassive Siberians with their bayonets dipped in pig fat.

Akulov said to Gunter in German, 'they nick your skin with these and you die poisoned. Think ahead so you avoid it SS. Traitors who live in hoops become poisoned like that interpreter. A bullet is the best cure for a traitor.'

Gunter said, 'you speak German?'

'And more languages but the interpreter didn't know.'

'He said you agreed to our contract.'

'He was correct, but the interpreter is dead in an hour. That leaves only you and me to remember the deal. Stay alive and think ahead in years. Reminders will come to jog your memory. Keep out of danger for us both, SS and use our favourite book to write to me when I ask.' He pushed Gunter over to the Siberians and went back to his headquarters.

Akulov went to the room where two NKVD soldiers waited with his sergeant and interpreter.

Akulov spat in the face of his interpreter and said, 'you fucking traitor,' and stood over him while the soldiers forced him to his knees.

'Negotiating with German prisoners is treason. Think about it while the sergeant puts some lead in your brain. Stay on your knees.' The sergeant fired a regulation bullet in the back of the interpreter's head.

*

Gunter's field commander listened to his report and accepted the coordinates for Russian artillery positions. He double-checked the location, called for his gunnery officer and handed them over. German shelling started at midnight and went on until dawn, focussed on Russian guns. At midday, an SS soldier was rescued from no man's land. Karl said he had hidden close to the Russian front line during the bombardment. His report indicated substantial military damage and loss of personnel. This was accurate, as Gunter's coordinates directed shells at a camp holding more than fifteen thousand captured German soldiers and most of them died that night.

Twenty-four hours later Russian artillery replied with their bombardment aimed at the German command headquarters. The boast of Russian accuracy was optimistic and their barrage went wide. Gunter's safe position was blasted by shells with a broad shrapnel pattern. Karl was wounded in both legs and Gunter in his back but the fine German drugs developed by SS doctors prevented infection. Front line warfare was over for them.

Their injuries sent them home to Germany with medals. SS soldiers wounded on the eastern front were heroes and deserved a bonus. They were assigned as concentration camp guards. Gunter never told Karl how his mind was destroyed in Russia and Karl never told Gunter how Akulov's sergeant put him in the chair to get the feel for things, before he took out a second Polish brain. Or, how he begged them not to do it to Gunter and swore allegiance to Akulov in return. Akulov owned them both. Neither Gunter nor Karl knew about the other's pact.

*

35

1944 Poland

Himmler wrote an edict saying he considered it..."*necessary to provide in the most liberal way, hard working prisoners in concentration camps, with women in brothels.*" Sex for labour. In his Auschwitz unit, Gunter supervised a brothel and that was difficult with so many cohabitation cells to look after. Starting out in the job it was amusing to watch the whores. The guards dodged from peephole to peephole. It got complicated when some men finished quickly and others never started. Himmler's rule laid down a maximum 20 minutes for sex in the horizontal position watched by a guard at the peephole. But a mother and son pairing was a challenge. It took time for papers and allocation vouchers to filter through before a woman could begin her special duties. Anna's papers made it clear she had permission to bring her son, Icy, but so far, there were no allocation vouchers. They desperately wanted whores for Himmler's incentive scheme but Anna couldn't start without her vouchers.

The path to death was an unemotional process and Gunter forgot how many Jews marched off rail transports direct to the gas chambers under his supervision. Job satisfaction in concentration camps was minimal from killing people who didn't resist. Work got tedious and pride was worn. A form of self-respect was sustained using mathematical precision to select Jews for extermination but supervision of a brothel was not mathematical like that. Himmler's directive insisted that commercial, not extermination purposes were pursued because the Third Reich had all it wanted for victory, except petrol. Here at Auschwitz was the finest petrochemical plant developed by the best brains in the west to convert coal into petrol. This section of Auschwitz existed to produce fuel for the German war machine. It used skilled labour and incentives for its slave workers.

'We do this to fuel our Panzers while Yanks drill holes in Texas and get oil,' said Karl.

Gunter replied, 'Germany has no oil and we need petrol to fight. Instead, these labourers make petrol from coal and our whores keep them working hard.'

Himmler's sexual reward system for outstanding work was simple and the administration was easy. Then in came a mother with her son and the boy sparked something in Gunter. He and the child shared the same material vacuum. Gunter paralleled with Icy because they both had nothing. To sway her into prostitution the hierarchy at Ravensbrück allowed Anna to bring her son to the brothel at Auschwitz and keep her beautiful hair. Icy created another dimension for its sexual bureaucracy.

In reality, the boy was an add-on Gunter could turn to ash with a pen's stroke. An adornment to a Polish whore sent to pleasure star workers. All the same, Gunter knew Icy would last and that he'd keep on further than his mother if it came to survival. Karl thought so too and said the child would see them all off. His aura demanded attention for if angels existed one sat on his shoulder. Except angels didn't exist in Auschwitz so Gunter began talking to Icy to learn their common ground and figure out what secrets a child had that intrigued him. They spoke in Polish at first but Icy picked up German words that Gunter used with the other guards. Soon they talked in German.

Their conversations were about children's things...how different foods might taste and about his mother. Icy looked at the insignia on Gunter's collar and asked him to explain what it meant. Symbols were important in Icy's world. He created them, and allocated them to people as supernatural playthings. They were his personal toys. Apart from the guards, everyone in the unit was a woman and Icy was not allowed to talk to them – only his mother. There were no books but Icy never seemed bored and used his fingers to create fantasy characters.

'What are those shapes?' Gunter said in Polish.

Icy made a figure with his hands, 'that is a man who wore a beautiful uniform and talked to my mother.'

'Show me another,' Icy moulded his fingers.

'Who is that?'

'It is you.'

'I can see,' said Gunter.

'And you have fire round your head,' Icy said in German.

'What do you mean by that?'

'My hands make your shape with fire round your head. I can't stop them.'

'Enough,' Gunter shivered.

Gunter's wooden hand puppets were the nearest thing to toys in the cohabitation unit and from the space outside his mother's cell, Icy watched Gunter whittle them to life. He created furniture and made a small rocking chair. Icy asked Gunter why it moved like it did.

'Will the chair fly?'

'It will feel like flying when you sit in it.'

'Can a puppet friend enjoy a ride with me?' said Icy.

'That would be nice,' said Gunter.

Just when it seemed the authorities had forgotten Anna, a package was delivered with his mother's name on it and Icy knew what it was when they opened it outside her cell door. Icy understood about the pile of vouchers for visits to his mother. They were tied with string.

Icy spoke in his childish German, 'Bitte hören Sie auf damit...*please stop this*,' and to calm him Gunter did.

The administrative logic of sex for labour was that hard-working men were rewarded with brothel women. The assignment for women was six months. Eight clients a day at 20 minutes a visit were stipulated. Enough vouchers were provided to cover these visits during a six-month period before return to Ravensbrück was authorised. Anna was ready for her shame. The unit held other women who were wrecked and they longed for it to happen to her. The SS masters at Ravensbrück named the prostitutes *Puff* women. After a day of sex, these women returned to their *Puff* hut but Gunter allowed Anna to stay with Icy in her cohabitation cell.

Gunter protected Anna but she knew things might change with a single visit because she could never refuse a client. Yet, men who came into her cell were speechless with fear and looked up at the peephole in the door for Gunter's SS eye to send them to the chambers. Word was passed between those who won visits. Anna was Gunter's private diversion. Camp information systems were efficient and Icy sat silent outside her door. The other women guessed about Anna's SS protector and tried to be friends but she spoke to no one but Icy. Women went out broken and mostly to die back at Ravensbrück where they'd been promised freedom for taking part in Himmler's sexual initiative. His promise was a lie. Anna marked off time.

Outside of his mother's cell, Icy waited for Gunter to speak.

'With hand puppets, use your face as a distraction for the audience.'

'You said keep my face like still water. What is a distraction?' said Icy.

'Fix the audience on your face then flash your eyes and return them to the puppets on your hands - they call that a distraction.'

'I can practise distraction.'

'Yes, guide your audience to see what *you* want them to see...then help them to see what *they* want to see.'

'What is this puppet's name?' said Icy.

'Gretel. Tomorrow you can have her for an hour.'

'She is very nice,' said Icy.

'There may be other puppets before you leave here.'

'Will they be beautiful like Gretel?'

'No, she is special,' said Gunter.

'Like my mother?'

'Yes.'

Each day Anna received men and collected her vouchers without sex. In dead time between visits, she tuned-in to the voices outside her cell and recognised the high-pitched timbre of Icy and the deeper tones of Gunter and sometimes those of Karl, her second protector. She heard Polish words spoken about wood and toys. Anna became dizzy with fear that she'd sold herself for nothing and gifted the life of her son as a plaything to the guards. Living was impossible in this state. Anna needed to know the truth but the penalty for speaking to a guard was 25 blows in the punishment cell.

She tried to discover Gunter's motives through Icy, whispered to her son in their wooden bed, and tried to explain what she must know. Icy understood and kissed his mother and put his arms around her neck and loved her. Anna could not comprehend that Gunter, the chief guard, was her son's language teacher and protector of a mother whore. She could not comprehend that Icy dictated what happened in her life while Gunter sent others to their death without a thought. Four months into Anna's sentence without sex, she understood the price of living was Icy.

Karl said, 'it's dangerous to play this game with her and the boy. She was sent to pleasure top workers and other women do her job as extra. There's gossip about why you protect those two.'

'All the women's vouchers come to me and it's interesting to watch him defend his mother.'

'He reminds you of the orphanage.'

'No.'

Karl said, 'he's got your knack for languages and you both talk with your hands.'

'Could be I'm getting soft and they should go to the chambers?'

'We had them tattooed. Prisoners for gassing don't get tattoos.'

Gunter smiled, 'those tattoos were your plan and maybe it's you who went soft. Leave things till they go back to Ravensbrück. She's done her six months soon and I have an idea.'

'They say Himmler went soft and ordered the release of prisoners from Ravensbrück.'

'That's right; thousands of women will go to Sweden as refugees and you can bet this mother and boy will be top of the list,' said Gunter.

'While we stay in this hole,' Karl was bitter.

'Listen to my idea and we have a chance to walk out of Ravensbrück with them,' said Gunter.

'How?'

'I hung on to the papers from those Polish brothers in Russia. We both speak Polish so I organised we join the Ravensbrück crowd due for release and walk out as prisoners. Mainly women are going with a few men mixed in. I know the date they open the gates and know the office boys who make things happen there. They can fix it for us to leave with a couple of their desk clerks that have the same idea but don't speak Polish. They want us for cover. We escort this mother and son with their bunch of six-month *Puff* colleagues from Auschwitz back to Ravensbrück and mix in there as prisoners. I arranged the escort duty back to Ravensbrück and the clerks arranged we walk out of there with their buddies plus a few thousand regular prisoners.'

'It's a long shot,' said Karl.

'We're losing the war.'

*

Anna sat on her cot suffocated by empty time when a new guard opened the door. Gunter was missing and Anna dared not speak. Icy sat outside. The guard said he heard she was lazy and had selected a prolific worker for her who'd exceeded all his targets. He laughed and said Anna must be flattered because this was the first Jew to be awarded sex for work at the petrol unit of Auschwitz. He stepped outside and pushed in a Jewish worker. It was Anna's husband, Dudel Warski.

The door slammed shut but its peephole stayed closed. The guard lost interest and left Dudel staring at the inside of the door. She said nothing and waited for him to turn around but he seemed dazed and leaned against the wall to gather strength. Anna whispered she thought he was dead and Dudel fixed his eyes on the door as if someone outside had called through it. She whispered again that she thought he was dead and he turned to look at her. Now he was dead because his mind circled inwards to his soul and he couldn't see her though he was face on.

She called his name but his spirit had left. Deserted by whatever god he believed in who allowed this to happen. No words could explain. She could not...he could not. They were just there. A client and whore. A man and wife. A Jew and Gentile. Cast together by fate for the greater cause of Germany and now hollowed out together. Whatever gave them life and hope before, vanished and left torment to flay the remnants. Twenty minutes went by without a word. Nothing was asked and nothing answered. They were voiceless while the quiet finished killing them. Destiny spared them to die wondering.

Outside the cell, there was shouting and Icy's shrill voice called out. She heard Gunter bellow in rage at the new guard and the door kicked open. Gunter brought his whip down full force on Dudel's shoulders and across his face until he dropped. Anna raised her arms but he lashed the yellow star on Dudel's shirt and shouted *"Jew, Jew,"* until Icy threw himself across Dudel and wrapped his arms round Gunter's leg.

    Icy screamed in German, 'das ist mein Vater...*this is my father,*' then clamped his teeth into the cloth of Gunter's trousers and held his leg tight in his childish arms. Gunter kicked to release the cloth from Icy's teeth but Icy held on and Gunter raised his whip. Anna screamed.

There was murder in Gunter's eyes and Anna believed someone must die to satisfy him. Gunter spoke in Polish and told Icy this man was a Jew. He could not be his father. Though she knew the consequences Anna said to him that they'd been married in Warsaw and he was Icy's stepfather. But the only word Gunter repeated was *"Jew"*. Dudel stirred on the floor and blood poured from the welt on his face. Icy took his teeth from Gunter's trousers and went to help him. It was as if Gunter had been shot when he saw the boy touch Dudel's face. He told Dudel to get outside and kicked him hard in the head so he rolled away and crawled out. Gunter told Anna if she spoke, he would send her to the chambers at the main camp. He made Icy sit on the bed and tell him everything.

'He gave us food and taught me to make shapes with my fingers and how to tear up paper for animals to dance on them,' said Icy.

'Are his hands clever?' said Gunter.

'Yes and he is clever with machines.'

Gunter said he knew a factory that employed Jews who were clever engineers. He might survive there and that was where Dudel was going. He glanced at Anna and her life was balanced by Icy then Gunter turned and slammed the door and she heard him walk away.

'What did father whisper to you on the floor?'

'Father said we should stay alive for him.'

36

The Caribbean - Tortola

Tuesday 16.45 - 22nd February 1966

Gassy dropped Gelson at the bar and walked to the dress shop to stretch his legs. Gunter sat amongst the scarves waiting for late customers. Gassy looked through the window.

'Did you leave the chair on the veranda at Meath's house?'

'Yes sir, I dropped the chair where you told me. Meath wasn't about. Guess he stayed at the airport.'

'That gets you fifty bucks,' Gunter held out a bill, 'Meath will ship it out for me with the pilot.'

Gassy reached through the window and took his money, 'not much business for dresses,' he said.

'Not much when it's late. How is it for you?'

'Jes picked up a guy at the airport that was drinking with Meath,' said Gassy.

'I saw a stranger there earlier. Mean looking white guy.'

'Could be dis man - kinda slow wid 'is dollars,' said Gassy flexing the thumb of his right hand to demonstrate.

'He in town?' said Gunter.

'Jes dropped him at the bar.'

'See you later.'

'Sure,' said Gassy.

*

When Gunter saw Gelson at the airport, he realised him and Meath were linked. They were the bodyguard-witnesses in balaclavas on the cay twenty-five ago...the two interpreters who spoke Spanish. Gelson's thumb gave them away. They should be dead but Gelson showed half a thumb to signal they were alive. Fritz told it right in 1941. Check their faces but that wasn't possible through balaclavas. For twenty-five years, Gunter believed his phosphorous grenade had vaporised all four men in the reception party. Coincidences dropped into place with Gelson's missing thumb and right away Gunter knew his wartime interpreters were alive and closing in. The dress shop was empty and Gunter unlocked the workroom door, rummaged under the varnishes and pulled out a first aid bag. Outside, the road was clear and Gunter settled down for his visitor to arrive.

*

The barman pointed Gelson to the dress shop and he went out looking for shade on the short walk. His battery and leads were heavy and he sweated. At the shop door, he adjusted his eyes to take in the rows of scarves and dresses in the gloom. Inside the shop, a wicker trunk rested on a trolley with rubber wheels used for delivering garments. Gelson walked in, put down his bag and looked over the side of the trunk. Then his nightmare started. It was dark but reality arrived when the chloroform wore off. His shoulders were pressed onto a hard surface and his mouth tasted of wood.

Gunter spoke to Gelson, 'you should be more careful with that hand, half a thumb is easy to remember but we can fix that.'

Gelson was naked, tied down with leather straps on the worktable and gagged and hooded. Gunter went into the shop, put on a long-playing record and turned up the sound then locked the place. It was closing time. When he got back to the workroom, Gelson was awake and struggled with the straps. Gunter arranged his instruments at the end of the worktable and positioned a mirror above Gelson's feet. He crouched near Gelson's head to check the reflection then pulled off his hood. Gunter tied a length of wire around Gelson's right wrist and tightened it to stop the flow of blood to his hand.

'Sure, we can fix that thumb,' Gunter said and severed it completely using a whittling knife. Gelson would have screamed but the sawdust stuffed in his mouth pushed the sound back into his throat and it was no louder than a sigh. Gunter sat on his chair and waited for him to stop fighting the straps.

When Gelson settled Gunter whispered, 'I want to get to know you and catch-up after all these years. Last time we met, you wore a balaclava but no gloves, and you with half a thumb even then. Now we fixed that problem. Like I was saying...we met on the cay twenty-five years ago and that's one thing to talk about but I need to find out what other memories come up.'

Gunter lifted Gelson's head, 'look in the mirror by your feet and you see the same as me. What I see are your balls.' Gunter slid a pillow under his head, 'this will help you watch me operate without straining.' Gunter picked up a scalpel and showed it to Gelson, 'after we met twenty-five years ago I got some easy work in camps. You know the sort of place. One assignment was to stop Jews breeding and my bosses' speciality was Jewish men. He trained us like this. A Jewish guy comes on a first visit and is strapped to a table, just like you. We never worried about anaesthetic or infection. On that first visit, the job was to remove one testicle...the second ball was for the second visit. What wore us down was the screaming when the first ball came off. I knew sawdust stopped that noise. You've got a mouth full of sawdust today and music to hear. Now watch in the mirror.'

Gunter marched to the other end of the table in step to the music and made an incision in Gelson's scrotal sac with the scalpel while he writhed and choked on his own screams. With a pair of scissors, Gunter removed his left testicle and held it up between his thumb and forefinger.

'What do they say about holding on to old skills?' and Gunter dropped the testicle in a dish. 'I want everything you know when you spew the sawdust. If you paint a full picture there's a chance you get out of here minus a ball and thumb. You still act coy we take the other ball. No sawdust, only music. If all that fails, you get a ride to the channel under the bridge and swim with sharks. You look tense. Spit the sawdust and start talking. Maybe some water to clear your throat.' Gunter untied the gag around Gelson's mouth, waited while he coughed up sawdust, and trickled water in his mouth.

When Gelson's breathing cleared Gunter said, 'tell it all.' Gelson told it all and Gunter listened to his story.

*

Gelson said when they left the cay in 1941, the principals decided their bodyguards should get lost when they opened the strongbox. In international waters, they sent Meath and Gelson below deck while they opened it with the combination number. Next thing, there's a bang and everything's on fire above. They grabbed some drinking water and went overboard for the dingy. The principals were vapour.

They floated in the dingy until a US destroyer picked them up and dropped them at the navy station in Puerto Rico. People waited for them including a woman from New York. She said her name was Martha Gold and asked a lot of questions to check their story. They weren't lying and back home him and Meath got retained by their corporations. For twenty years, they got sent to different places, to look out for the guy who made the drop on the cay. Finally, they got told Tortola was the real deal where you and your stuff were located. Right back where it started in '41.

Gunter fingered the scalpel and asked why so many people suddenly knew where he was. Gelson said he never knew personally but three years before, Meath was hauled in by the FBI to check out the story of a Russian defector. Meath's boss told him to go. One FBI interrogator at the interview was Martha Gold - the woman from 1941 who met them in Puerto Rico. She told Meath the defector was a communist intelligence officer who claimed he knew things about Meath and me and why our party went to the cay in '41. She must've had inside information from Meath's boss so he played along. The FBI needed to check if his information was true because this guy was desperate to stay in America and selling anything. He swore he knew about your stuff to keep from getting sent back to Russia.

'He swore what?' said Gunter.

'He swore you told him you made a switch on the cay in 1941 and we sailed away with buttons. He knew what you took was near here but not exactly where it was hidden.'

Gunter said, 'keep talking.'

Gelson said, 'this Martha woman asks Meath to hear the Russian's story with just the three of them together. She pulls rank and the other agents leave. Martha wants to check out it's not bullshit so he can stay in America. Meath hears him out and tells Martha it's accurate. Then her Russian says you'd vamoose if you picked up a bad smell. Martha didn't care for Meath to hear this and tells him to forget it. She asks Meath if the Russian's story stacks up one hundred percent about the drop at the cay in '41. Meath says it stacks up fine but the only guy who knows where to find the stash is the guy who hid it - *you*.'

'Then what happened?'

'Nothing, as far as me and Meath are concerned until we're told to find you and the goods out here. We get told to pull no punches. But, after Meath's interview he sees a picture of this Martha broad in a newspaper. Not much is said except she's under investigation for breaches of security. Later, Meath sees a piece in the same paper that she's been found dead in her apartment. Charges of selling classified information have been made against her. Meath buys all the papers and checks their stories about Martha. One paper said she peddled FBI stuff to Israel and another said to Britain. A couple of days later there's a story Martha got paid by US corporations as a freelance, and then nothing more. Both Meath and me know who the corporations might be, but soon the papers are printing apologies about this slur on American business and it goes dead. These corporations are big players with big money and big friends in Congress. We guess they've leaned on the story and it's not worth the trouble for the papers to run it. Not long after, we're briefed by our security people on where to look for you but told to stay out of sight until they press the button. Nobody knows for sure you're the real guy. Now, I guess I know you are. They figure there's other interested parties because they heard Martha shared her information with Israel and Britain. Like us, they want the stuff and like us, they don't know where it's stashed. But what they all want more than anything are the receipts Meath and me countersigned. Until now, the gloves were on, but we were sent bare-knuckle signals before the others got to you. That's why it went hot this week.'

Gunter teased the scalpel and Gelson said, 'that's everything.'

'What was the name of this Russian?'

'Meath said the dame called him Akulov.'

'And the FBI dame again?' said Gunter.

'Martha Gold. She was a Jew.'

'We go to a safe place with no more surgery,' Gunter said and sprinkled drops of chloroform on the gauze, 'and you leave when The Royal visit is finished.' Gelson breathed hard when he placed the gauze on his face.

Gunter dragged the garment trunk and wheels to the workroom door and unstrapped Gelson. He tied his hands and feet with parcel tape, filled his mouth with sawdust, and pulled a gag tight. Gelson was heavy and it took all his strength to lift him into the trunk but it pushed smoothly into the shop. Gunter dropped in the battery and leads. He covered Gelson with dresses and chose a black outfit and hat as the last items in for his personal disguise. He washed his instruments and tidied the workroom. Finally, he inspected the ring of puppets on the wall and took down his favourite. Gunter sat Gretel on the lid of the trunk, pushed it out of the door, and headed for home. Heat kept the streets deserted and the trolley's rubber wheels were noiseless on the level ground. Gretel rested easy on top.

Gunter spoke to Gretel while he pushed the trunk.

'For twenty-five years, Meath and his friend Gelson vanish and now they float up. Next, the soldier Jayce steals my invite from Himmler. The only reward Germany gave me and Jayce thieves it after he got fucked. He's dead for that but tell me who controls him? And where is B6174 with his white hair and who directed him here? We will recognise them all when they show their hand. They know me but can't find what I hid and must parade themselves to find that. We have a fifty-fifty chance to escape with our dollars and diamonds, Gretel. Better than most chances me and you had in life.'

While Gunter spoke to Gretel he marched at full pelt but slowed his pace when Rudolph stepped out of the shadows.

'Take the Frenchman's powerboat and anchor off Meath's house tomorrow with fuel to reach my place in town and then St Thomas after that. You've booked an appointment to meet Jayce on the beach when

The Queen opens her bridge. Stay put until I cross the bridge wearing the black dress and hat you want for your mother. You get the clothes when I get to the sand and we head off in the powerboat.' Rudolph slipped into the shadows but Gunter called after him as he moved away, 'if I'm late, wait at my house and you still get the dress and hat.' Rudolph raised his hand to acknowledge the instruction and vanished in the night.

Gunter said to Gretel, 'greed is easy to understand. Rudolph cheats me and greed makes him bright. He cheats Jayce and it does the same. But, Rudolph loves a double cross more than greed because he enjoys his own cleverness, which tempts him to drop caution. It's careless to mislay caution when you engage with a master puppeteer whose line of work is deceit. Tomorrow, Rudolph's greed will bring Jayce into my gun sight and you can enjoy the kill. Then Rudolph will drive his boat to town and die with me...or so it will appear. Be calm, that's how it will look, except Rudolph will die with Gelson. Rudolph comes to my house with greedy thoughts and that will kill them both. After that, we can relax and leave for a new life. Gelson will give silent testimony that it was me who died and our enemies will give up the chase for my hidden treasure. Sshh Gretel - we don't want Gelson to know he will pass away as a German soldier in my place.

37

The Caribbean - Tortola

Wednesday 09.00 - 23rd February 1966

Gunter turned off the road and hid his car behind a derelict sugar store. He pulled on the black, full-length dress taken from the trunk at his house, smoothed out the creases and put on the hat. It was cool and he settled the gun case under his left arm, picked up the bouquet of flowers, and wedged his puppet amongst the blooms. He walked up the drive to the big house. Guests were expected later, but it was quiet now. Across the courtyard, a track led to Old Sarah's shack. Gunter crossed the courtyard and went up the track holding his dress to keep it from snagging on thorn bushes.

Henry watched Gunter climb the drive to the courtyard of the big house carrying his gun case and the bouquet of flowers from San Juan. A breeze blew Gunter's dress about his legs. Within an hour, the first guests arrived and parked their cars. Henry waited until a dozen people went up the drive to the house and climbed after them. Gunter was trapped until the celebrations ended and these people left. Guests packed the courtyard and dozens more arrived to grab drinks and dance to the music. This once-in-a-lifetime visit by The Queen, justified a party.

*

Gunter pushed the door of the shack open. The cat was somewhere on the hillside and would come. There was a smell of petrol from the can under the chair. He went outside and laid the bouquet of flowers on the graves then went back in and sat Gretel on the window ledge. Piece by piece, he assembled the rifle, fixed on the silencer and scanned the bridge with the ZF-4 telescopic site. For a sniper waiting came easy and the day wore on. Sounds drifted up from the courtyard where drinkers jostled for viewing positions of the Royal party. Gunter traversed the bridge and followed the beach round to the veranda of Meath's house. There were hours to wait and he talked to Gretel on the window ledge.

'As a child you made friends with a boy who had special hands. This boy and his mother used Polish names that were easy to forget but their number was 6174. They had white hair. B6174 was his tattoo and I feel him here. In those days at Auschwitz, he was an infant but his eyes killed you at snipers range. I know his eyes are on us. You were his favourite puppet and we had nice times together. I looked after him and his mother and kept that Jew stepfather alive. Look out for our clever Polish boy.'

Gunter slipped the puppet on his left hand and moved her about.

'You may dance on my gun when Jayce is dead. The British were not so clever to trap me with a soldier but they are smart enough to give him a sly controller we don't see. It doesn't matter who that is because nobody can find us on the mountain. Even more stupid are the greedy Americans that sent Meath and Gelson to find me after twenty five years. Gelson told us their story. By tomorrow, they will all believe me to be dead.

*

At 12.10, well-known faces strolled across the bridge as if they were on their way home after a day at the office. Their lips moved in silent conversation. The noise of music carried up the mountain to Gunter from the courtyard. The Queen's face was big in the gun sight...haughty and talking with the black man beside her. Gunter moved his scope from her eyes to the centre of her forehead and down to her mouth, which moved soundlessly. What did she say? What was there to say about a bridge that took five minutes to open? A bird landed behind The Queen. Gunter blew its head off with a shot, and it fell in the channel for the sharks. The gun was accurate, silent, and ready for Jayce.

Gunter's black dress rode up when he crouched in the firing stance. His outfit was finished off with a jaunty hat worn by an old woman out to watch The Queen. It was appropriate to mete out death wearing black. Gunter settled back against the window frame with the crossed hairs steady on the target. It was sad to make a head shot and spoil the features and he preferred a chest shot to break the spinal column. Gretel looked on as Gunter rested the FG 42 on the window frame.

*

The Doctor sat at the airport bar. Meath served a glass of milk to a white-haired man.

'Hi doc,' said Meath.

'Where is everybody?' said The Doctor.

'At the bridge, I guess.'

'Was Rudolph here?'

'He went to the Frenchman's place, but it's closed,' said Meath.

'Everywhere is closed for The Queen's visit.'

'We still have to make a living,' Meath nodded to his solitary customer, 'or I'd watch The Queen do her stuff from my house.'

The Doctor glanced at Icy, 'tell him he'll burn in the sun with his white skin.'

'I'll tell him. You want a drink?'

'No,' The Doctor walked across to the restaurant.

The door was open and The Doctor went through to the dining area. Rats scampered in the roof but the tables were empty and he sat down. Italia touched his arm.

'Are you looking for Jayce?'

'Yes.'

'He went to meet Rudolph.'

'Where?'

'At Meath's house. Rudolph took the Frenchman's powerboat,' said Italia.

'Show me how to get there.'

'Follow the line of palms and walk on the beach.' Italia took him onto the porch and pointed to a gap in the trees, 'or there is a trail through the mangrove swamp that Meath uses to drive home from his bar. The beach is quicker for you and Jayce went that way.'

The Doctor ran through the trees and stumbled onto the beach. He thought of Jayce crumpling a picture of The Queen into a ball and pushed his body to greater speed. His low profile shoes churned the sand and he ran with the sea on his left. Jayce insisted his cover on the island was believable. But to get sexually close to Gunter involved more than a good story. London said Jayce had perfect qualifications for the honeytrap but he'd gone out of control. The Doctor knew the situation was dangerous because an unhinged agent wasn't accountable.

*

Rudolph pressed against the wall of Meath's house and heard a thin voice carry on the wind but the words blew out to Buck Island in the distance. He couldn't put a direction to it so hugged the wall and fixed his eyes on Jayce getting close. Jayce recognised The Doctor's voice behind him and jogged faster, keeping tight into the trees. At 12.15 pm, The Royal Party had crossed the bridge when he arrived at Meath's house. Rudolph avoided his eyes.

Jayce said, 'you told me to meet you here and you'd bring the papers with the Nazi emblem I drew for you?' Rudolph stayed silent. 'You promised to get them but I can see you've got nothing. Gunter's place was easy to search today when he closed for the Royal celebrations. I said find his papers and get rich. Four receipts with a picture on top and things were fixed for your mother. A bonus if you found more. The Doctor has plenty of money to pay for everything.' Jayce looked hard at Rudolph, 'something's wrong…you didn't get them and still showed up. You must have come for a reason.' Rudolph looked away but there was nothing to gain from threatening him.

Jayce stepped onto the beach to catch sight of the Royal visitors. The Queen and Duke of Edinburgh had crossed the bridge and were about to get in a car on the road to his right. For a moment Jayce enjoyed his proximity to the couple and then his mind went back to Rudolph's motive for meeting him here. The answer came in a whisper of death from Gunter's rifle on the mountain. The bullet struck him in the chest and broke his spine before it exited. There was no pain but the impact lifted him across the beach and his lungs filled with blood. Jayce was dying. The

Doctor's cry on the wind was closer and Jayce forced staccato phrases out to Rudolph.

'The Doctor will pay you - for those papers - with the swastika - go to Gunter's house - take papers to The Doctor - he has money.' The last of Jayce's blood drained into the sand while The Queen drove off to The Royal Yacht Britannia.

The Doctor's head was down, struggling for breath and he ran hard along the beach. As he got close to Meath's house, Rudolph worked his way around the back and stayed hidden. The Doctor saw Jayce lying on the sand and searched for a pulse in his wrist but life had gone so there was urgent work to do. The Doctor had lost his agent and it was unforgiveable in their secret world to leave evidence. His agent was dead and so was his nephew. The Doctor's intelligence career was finished. He checked Jayce's pockets, took out his wallet and dropped it on the sand. Then he dragged Jayce into the sea without looking at his face. The Doctor said a prayer as his nephew sank out of sight. The Frenchman's powerboat bobbed in the waves but there was no sign of Rudolph. He picked up the wallet and went back along the beach. The Royal couple had gone and the bridge was empty.

*

When the revellers moved to the edge of the courtyard to watch The Royal party, Henry hid in the guest cottage. Gunter was cornered further up the mountain in Sarah's shack and that left him plenty of time. Henry's deadline was dusk, and his only escape route was across the bridge to the airport. From sunset tonight to dawn tomorrow, the twenty-seven foot lifting span was raised isolating Beef Island and the airport from the main island. After sunset, the only way to escape was swim the channel with hammerhead sharks. Sunset was 18.21, moonrise 18.43 and moonset 21.05. Henry memorised the times from air traffic control as escape windows for him and Icy.

Late in the afternoon, the white woman came in the door and looked old, edged by sunlight. Music spilled through the open door. She pushed it shut and turned the lock.

'Everyone has left. In fifteen minutes you can go too,' she said.

'I need to go now.'

She said, 'no,' and pressed his hand to her breast, 'payment is owed for your mysterious request to keep the music playing for thirty minutes after you leave.'

'I'll explain the joke tomorrow,' said Henry, but there was no joke about his request. With music playing, Gunter must assume people were still in the courtyard and his route past the house from Sarah's shack was blocked. That gave Henry thirty minutes to get up the mountain but first, the host required fifteen minutes to pay for her favour. Time was running out.

38

The Caribbean - Tortola

Wednesday 17.00 - 23rd February 1966

Through his sniper's scope Gunter watched Meath talk to a man with white hair. The man was tied with rope in Gunter's rocking chair, on the veranda of Meath's house. His head was lowered and they were near a charcoal brazier to keep off insects. The white haired man wore a long sleeved shirt and Meath did a strange thing and rolled up the sleeves. When Meath stepped away, Gunter saw a black mark on the inside of the man's arm but it was too far for detail. His white hair fell back when he looked up and Gunter saw child B6174 grown into a man. His protégé from Auschwitz whose number and hair Italia described. Another agent who Gelson told him was somewhere about. Like a chick pecking through the shell of consciousness, his name came to mind - *Ignacy Czeberowski*. Icy, the grown man, finally sat in Gunter's full sized rocking chair.

*

Meath talked with a lit Marlborough hanging from his bottom lip.

'I never figured out who wanted the same stuff as me but you got careless at dusk yesterday. Sometimes I take a nap behind the bar when there ain't no customers. You were loose-mouthed when you nattered to your friend after the flight and said you had it all worked out about the

German. Told the pilot to do his job and leave the secret stuff to you. There's me lying still as a corpse not three feet away and you spill the beans but didn't say what you'd worked out. Me and you both know we want what the German hid. You figured out where it's hid and now you're gonna tell me. Easy or painful you'll talk.' Icy held his head down and said nothing. Meath took the cigarette from his bottom lip and stared at the white hair.

It was too far away for Gunter to hear what Meath said. Silent as his puppet shows at the orphanage. Meath pressed both of Icy's arms with the tip of his cigarette. He shouted something but Icy never moved with the burns. Icy was tough and Gunter felt the pain worse. He wouldn't talk because Gunter knew how Icy the child fought for his mother in the brothel and that took willpower. "Bitte hören Sie auf damit...*please stop this,*" his childish cry leaped from an Auschwitz brothel into Gunter's mind.

Meath threatened with his cigarette but Icy looked at him and said nothing. Then Meath went in the house and came back with a beer. In his other hand, he held a pair of tongs and said something but Icy shook his head. Meath went to the brazier, stirred the hot charcoal with the tongs, and sipped his beer. Everything was still until Meath went behind the chair and rocked it forward so it burned Icy's face in the coals. Icy's little voice from Auschwitz whispered again… "Bitte hören Sie auf damit…*please stop this,"* and Gunter went motionless with the gun. Meath stood upright and spread his arms. He laughed and walked round the chair to look at Icy's burned face. Gunter shot Meath in the head at the same range he'd killed Jayce. Through his scope he saw Meath's brain blow into Icy's face.

*

After sex, Henry got out fast carrying his shoulder bag and jacket. When the white woman closed the front door to the main house, he ran across the courtyard to the track leading to Sarah's shack. The sun was lower and he climbed through the pain in his foot. Music from the courtyard muffled his approach and ten feet from the shack, Henry dropped his bag and jacket. He froze when Gunter spoke in a voice flecked with laughter. Henry waited for another voice but there was no answer and Gunter began talking again. Henry calculated he could be at the side of the shack in less than four strides. Who was the other person inside?

While Gunter talked, Henry scampered across and pressed his ear to the wall. A chair scraped on the floor and the voice stopped. Gunter hummed a tune and Henry followed the sound to the window where he'd seen his face through the Frenchman's telescope. Gunter carried a rifle then and must have it now. Inching along the wall Henry peered round the corner of the building and saw a gun barrel on the window ledge pointing at the bridge. Henry needed to grab it to stand a chance in a close fight. Icy told him to make the hit using his preferred way of killing.

Henry turned the corner and grabbed the barrel and pressed his cheek against it. Gunter had one eye to the telescopic sight and the other stared at him in disbelief. Henry locked the barrel tight with both hands.

'What a pleasure,' said Gunter raising his head from the sight, 'but an unexpected actor in our drama.'

'The barrel's warm,' said Henry, 'who did you shoot?'

'Jayce was my British target, though I believe his uncle survives him. So, you must belong to the Jewish camp?'

'Maybe,' Henry put his weight on the barrel to fix it in place against the window ledge.

'And your master is B6174?'

'You've never seen him,' said Henry.

'Possibly a fleeting glance and the number's familiar.' Gunter dragged on the rifle stock to break Henry's grip.

'Did you shoot Icy?'

'Icy...you mean B6174? No.'

They were eye to eye in a test of strength over the gun. Gunter's stare transfixed him and Henry's grip on the barrel slackened. Then a puppet with a wooden head smashed Henry's face from his right side. The blow broke the lock of Gunter's eyes and Henry gripped the barrel tighter. Gunter tried to pull the gun away but failed and smashed Henry's face again with the puppet and inched the barrel towards him.

'This is Gretel,' said Gunter. The doll moved closer on Gunter's left hand ready for a knockout blow, but her movement broke his hypnotist's spell. Henry snatched harder at the barrel to pull Gunter close and their faces touched. The puppet flashed at him and her nose gouged Henry's right eyebrow. The two men cracked heads but Henry ignored the attack because it was a diversion. The gun in Gunter's right hand was the killing tool.

For a heartbeat their eyes met and Gunter took on the look of a man who saw a friend. Henry waited for the smile to follow. Gretel came again with a strike from his right and Henry let go of the barrel to escape Gunter's unblinking presence. Gunter pulled the gun towards him and traversed the muzzle to point at Henry. He was slowed by Gretel on his left hand but certain of victory. Now that Henry had released the barrel, there was no hurry to shoot.

The stillness of a professional killer enfolded Henry and the molecules of his being gathered into a primeval force. Henry's trademark was face-on murder and Icy said he was the best. Face-on murder called for style under pressure and Henry stayed alive because he was more elegant than those he killed. Gunter moved the barrel in a leisurely arc. There were a couple of seconds left before the black muzzle centred on his chest and Henry rose on his toes like a matador. He choreographed the ballet of his kills in milliseconds.

Henry said, 'I'll give Icy your regards,' and in a half turn and flash of light on steel, pulled the fish knife from the sheath round his neck and stabbed it deep into Gunter's right eye. It went through to his brain for an instant kill. Gunter slumped against the window ledge in the sniper's position with his gun pointing at the bridge. Henry pulled the knife from his eye. It was a trademark hit. Icy said nobody used a blade to the face like him because it took real nerve. Henry knew they died fast that way.

Henry backed away from the window. Gunter was his final hit and now, there was only the escape to consider. As he turned from the window, the bushes rustled and an animal leaped at him and he swiped with his fish knife but missed the creature that raked his arm with razor claws. The cat sprang at his face, clawing his cheek and blood ran into his shirt collar. It came again but he sidestepped and swung upwards with his knife and disembowelled the animal. Still the cat pulled back to fight for Gunter but its life was draining away. Henry smashed a rock on the cat's head until its brain showed white. He threw the body through the window into the shack. The music stopped in the courtyard of the big house.

The sun was sinking but the road to the bridge was still blocked with people. Henry's face and arm were in too much of a mess to get through the crowd and over the bridge. He limped down the track with his shoulder bag and crossed the empty courtyard to the drive. He needed help. Without a plane and his flying skills, him and Icy were trapped. There was no way out for them except by air and here on British territory, goodwill was short for Mossad killers. Ignoring the pain in his foot, Henry went to call in his favour from The Doctor.

*

Gunter stared one-eyed out of the window in his black dress. Daylight was fading when The Doctor lit a candle stub and melted some wax to fix it on the chair in Sarah's shack then blew out the flame. Gunter was frozen in the sniper's position and he pulled his chin off the window ledge and looked into one blue and one red eye. He laid him on the floor alongside the cat and the heater that was overturned as if by accident.

Gunter's pockets were empty and The Doctor tore a strip from the hem of the dress, rolled his body flat, and sliced his wrists to leave a suicide clue for the post mortem. He splashed petrol onto the walls of the shack and sprinkled a few drops on the strip of material torn from the dress. Using his thumb, he pressed one end of the strip into the tacky wax at the base of the candle, and ran the other end to the fabric covering Gunter's legs. The strip of material was a homemade fuse.

He poured petrol over Gunter, soaking his dress and head. Gunter's funeral pyre ignited when the stub burned down to the strip of material, and then to the dress. All to make it seem like Henry committed suicide and the cat knocked over the stove to cause the fire. Nights grew cold in February but petrol fumes were unpredictable so he got out quick with the gun and case after he re-lit the candle.

The Doctor dropped Henry's jacket well clear of the shack. It left plain evidence that Henry's body was inside. He picked Gunter's flowers off the graves and went down the track to the big house. Lights were on inside and he laid the flowers outside the front door and printed on the florist's card:

I CAN'T LIVE WITHOUT YOU – HENRY

He knocked on the door and waited in the shadows. The white woman looked out, saw the flowers and took them in with Henry's suicide note. The Doctor stumbled down the drive to the road and started his car. He raced home to pull Henry out of the rancid, underground tank of water where he floated in the dark.

*

Rudolph moored the Frenchman's powerboat in town and went to Gunter's house. Jayce said The Doctor would pay well for documents with a Nazi logo. Rudolph used a screwdriver to break the lock of Gunter's front door. He levered it into the soft wood of the frame to spring the catch. There was resistance when he pushed the door open a few inches so he pressed harder and the house exploded. If Rudolph had gone through the back door, he'd have seen an elegant bomb. A detonator and dynamite were attached by a simple pulley to the inside handle of the front door. When it opened wide the primary explosive triggered a secondary blast from portable gas bottles arranged neatly around Gelson. He sat upright in a hard backed chair, tied with parcel tape and his screams were choked by sawdust.

*

Henry arrived at his rendezvous with Icy on the veranda of Meath's house.

'There ain't much of a moon,' Icy said without moving.

'No,' said Henry.

'We fly the Beech to San Juan, ready for the laundry tomorrow,' said Icy.

'You tied in a rocking chair with a burned mug. Fuck the laundry.'

'I never heard ya swear much,' said Icy. Henry laid Meath's beer can on Icy's face.

'Gunter is dead. Stabbed through the eye the way you knew I'd do it,' said Henry.

'Face-on ya the best with a knife - but the bridge is raised?'

'I swam the channel,' said Henry.

'Lucky for you the sharks took a nap.'

'The Doctor saved my skin.'

'Why'd British opposition do that?'

Henry untied Icy and helped him to stand, 'said he owed me for pulling Jayce out of the reef cave.'

'Then he's OK,' said Icy.

'He told me Jayce was killed.'

'Too bad.'

'Me and you are all square now?'

'Yeah, our contract is settled kid.'

'OK,' said Henry.

'We get the fuck outta here pronto. I got news for those Israeli powers that jerk my strings. Ya don't need involvement with them kid. Play dead,' said Icy.

'I'm dead on the mountain,' said Henry, 'that's another thing The Doctor fixed.'

'Put the chair in Meath's jeep and drive to the airport,' said Icy.

'Wait till I sink his body in the swamp.'

'That was some shot you got him with. I always knew you as a knife man.' Henry ducked down and took hold of Meath's foot.

'It wasn't difficult with a rifle,' Henry dragged the body across the veranda.

'Watch out, the swamp is real dark.'

Henry paused, 'when I got off the mountain, The Doctor hid me in his underground water tank with fish and a million crawling bugs. It was hell with the lid shut tight. I know plenty about darkness.' Henry kicked Meath off the edge of the veranda and vanished in the mangroves dragging the body behind him.

'But ya blew Meath's head off before the lights went out for me,' Icy said to himself. He went in the house to get a cold beer for his face, then lugged the rocking chair to the jeep and waited for Henry.

*

Both Pratt and Whitney engines roared loud and Henry went through his usual pre flight checks but taxied without using lights. He turned to face down the length of the runway and dropped the tail wheel lock into position on the Beech D18S.

'Icy, this is my last takeoff from Beef Island so listen while I kill time. When we arrived in '64, they had 8,500 passengers pass through here on a 2,000-foot strip. Until the bridge was finished last month, everything crossed the channel on a hand-drawn pontoon. Today, the bridge was opened and suddenly us two are history. Ok, I'm bullshitting you with information to keep your mind off the pain.'

'This ain't your usual direction to fly-off the island,' said Icy, 'it's sure black out there.'

'That's right, but watch for a fire ahead in the night sky and when you see it, hold your rocking chair steady for takeoff.'

'Sure,' said Icy.

'The Doctor will light a beacon that stands-in as my funeral pyre and makes me officially dead. Without that steer we could hit the mountain.'

'Ya fill me with confidence.'

'This was our final mission and I'm careful.'

'With us both?'

'Yes, with us both. Keep the beer can on your face.'

'Nobody's gonna stop us,' said Icy.

Henry finished his checks and waited for the fire on the mountain to guide them on takeoff. When the candle burned down to the vein of black material leading to the dress, fire spread to Gunter's legs and body until it reached his head where it hesitated. Then, with a quiet roar, it billowed candescent and lit the reservoir of petrol in his mouth. Flames licked the tinder walls and the shack became a beacon as the wood ignited.

*

The Doctor threw Gunter's gun and case into the sea on his way to meet Italia and parked behind the bar where she waited for him. The Doctor pulled the jukebox plug and took her hand.

'You look beautiful,' he said.

'Thank you.'

Italia picked up a sound in the night and pointed to the sky. The roar of air-cooled, radial engines drifted across the bridge to the bar.

'He is leaving?'

'Yes.'

'Was there a message?'

'Expect a letter.'

'In our time together he spoke many words – a letter won't help.'

'He loved you, but Henry's work is complicated. He said have the baby.'

'That is hard to believe.' Italia wept.

'It's what he said,' The Doctor was lying.

The engine noise grew louder until the plane turned away from its flaming beacon and vanished in the night sky.

'He cared for you in his own way.'

'Not enough to stay.'

'Some things are hard to understand.'

'Henry is gone.'

'People will say he's dead.'

'And so, can never return.'

'Henry left a baby inside you to love,' said The Doctor.

Outside the bar, excited voices talked of the fire at Old Sarah's shack on the mountain.

*

The Doctor dropped Italia at the Frenchman's restaurant and went home. He eased off his rubber shoes to stretch out on the chair. As an afterthought, he went to the fridge for a Maserati to lighten his mood but hesitated when a car pulled up outside and then heard footsteps on the patio.

'Doctor,' said Italia, 'something happened at the restaurant and I caught a taxi straight here,' she was distressed, 'I must speak with you.' Her tone of voice told him he needed a drink.

His hand shook when he reached in the cupboard for a glass and it slipped from his fingers. Italia jumped from the shower of crystal.

'Let me clear it away,' she took a brush. The Doctor picked up another glass while Italia swept the floor.

She held up a length of wire, 'this was under your fridge.'

'I don't think it's important,' but twisted the wire with his fingers.

'Be careful of your feet.'

'Yes,' said The Doctor.

'Put on your shoes against the glass.'

'Of course.'

The Doctor stared at the refrigerator. Was it the cold home of Maseratis or haven of a gift from Jayce? He pressed the release button on the handle, opened the door a fraction and put his eye to the gap. Wire was taped to the inside of the door with enough slack to tighten when it was half-open. The wire ran to a paper bag on the shelf below the bowl of Maserati. Neat and dangerous. The Doctor's heart thumped and he opened the door six inches, unpeeled the tape and coiled the wire. He removed the pencil detonator that protruded from the bag to defuse the booby trap, and laid it on the shelf. Once separated, the explosive and detonator were harmless.

The Doctor whispered into the fridge, 'a great deal of hatred is needed to kill an uncle but your target was off beam. Military powers in Whitehall sent you to Gunter's bedroom, not me. You came out of the closet, accepted the challenge with pleasure and then took cover in self-loathing. Which of us is the lucky one Jayce? Time will tell if opening the refrigerator might have served me better. A scrap of wire swept up by Italia rang no alarm without Henry's warning in the hospital. One way or another Henry saved us both so I was right to be chivalrous, reciprocate the favour, and help him escape. Whitehall might take a dim view of this.'

The Doctor filled his glass and poured a small drink for Italia.

'Sip it.'

'I must go away.'

'No.'

'The Frenchman told me to leave; he knows I am with child.'

'You need a place to stay.'

'I will go home to my mother.'

'Do something for me Italia?'

'My answer to you will always be *yes*.'

'Marry me?'

'Why?'

'To save my soul.'

'I don't love you.'

'We might learn about love.'

'I carry another man's child.'

'You'll need help with a baby.'

*

Henry coasted off the main runway at San Juan International Airport, and parked by the customs shed. A loader put the rocking chair and Henry's bag on his trolley and took it inside. Icy palmed a hundred dollars to the Puerto Rican customs officer who chalked the seat of the chair to clear it.

Icy said, 'I'll come back for the chair after this guy checks in for his flight.'

'Clean him up in the washroom first,' the officer said, 'try some dry clothes.'

'He looks bad?'

'Your face is worse.'

Henry said, 'a hundred bucks is too much to smuggle in a rocking chair for your girl.'

'It's not just for her; I wanted it to remind me of what we did together.'

Henry laughed, 'we did a few things together Icy.'

'Listen kid...about the money coming your way.'

'Our contract is finished.'

'You get extra for Meath,' said Icy.

'I'm a contract hitter and we're square.'

'Our deal was stitched in Beirut. Meath pays extra.'

'You owe me nothing.'

'I owe a bonus now ya officially dead with zero income from hits. Don't sneeze at the dough.'

'Make it right for Italia,' said Henry, 'that's a bonus.'

'I promised to do that anyhow.'

'My night flight leaves for New York in a while and I need to clean up.'

'Take the money kid. There was a load came in with our cover.'

Henry hesitated, 'there won't be another controller like you.'

Icy stuffed an envelope in Henry's shirt pocket, 'your women never kept you faithful like me.'

'None of them had the class to pick me up outside a Beirut cemetery.'

'Twenty grand in dollar bills is a class bonus.'

'Jesus.'

'*Jesus*...show respect to a pretend Jew. And the rocking chair is *my* bonus.'

Icy pressed his lips tight as Henry limped off but after a few steps he turned back.

'This was our big play Icy and I guess it meant a lot to you.'

'Yeah, it meant a lot. Plus there were links with a place where I grew up...kinda hard to explain this late about a camp.'

'Like a Palestinian refugee camp?'

'Something close, but this place was mostly for Jews.'

'I almost forgot to leave your present,' Henry took a puppet from his shoulder bag, 'Gunter had this little woman with him at the shack and she belted me with her head. It has my blood on it and her dress is damp from the channel swim. She and Gunter were some pair...almost as good as you and me.'

'Her name is Gretel.'

*

The Caribbean police sifted through evidence of two deaths that happened on the 23rd of February 1966. At the first investigation, experts might have detected a controlled explosion but there were no experts. The front door of Gunter's house was blown to matchwood and Rudolph was impaled by splinters and killed. Identification of Gunter relied on body parts but the police were certain it was him. Strange that so much parcel tape was mixed in. An officer found a hand with its thumb blown off in the accidental gas explosion.

At the second investigation, police found a charred body under the ashes that had been Old Sarah's shack. It was impossible to identify the corpse, but the contents of a jacket provided conclusive evidence it was Henry. There was no next of kin to give it to after the inquest. A white woman supplied Henry's suicide note. She was respectable and not his usual type.

*

39

The Caribbean - San Juan

Thursday 12.00 - 24th February 1966

Michael arrived with two Israeli security men but sniffed at Icy's offer of a ride in a vibrating chair.

'Turn ya nose up at the chairs but they make more dough than those carpets in Beirut,' said Icy.

'What happened to the other money you made in the Caribbean sun?' said Michael.

'It got spent on the best cover for me and cost Israel nothing.'

'That's your business, Icy. We came to hear the real story, not about money.'

'Squeeze in this chair Michael and rock yourself calm.'

Icy said there was a lot to talk about and asked if the expert from Israel had arrived. Michael said he was in a hotel near the apartment and Icy said call him over now. Michael used the phone and in fifteen minutes, the expert arrived.

Icy sat the two security men in vibrating chairs and said leave the switches alone when you make notes. They used notebooks with yellow paper. Michael's face was tense and he said there was crazy radio traffic from Tel Aviv since yesterday's action because people were nervous there. Their intelligence service, Mossad, wanted to know about casualties. Icy told him who was dead and when it came to Gunter and Henry, he told the story again. The security men asked for it a third time and wrote down that Gunter and Henry were dead on their yellow paper.

Icy said, 'think of the difference between Gunter and Henry, because both these guys were killers. One of them killed Jews in the war and the other killed whoever I told him to in the name of Jews. When I talk like that, the lines are blurred and I gotta remind myself of this kid recruited in Beirut. He thinks I saved him and maybe he's right but he still died. The German had qualities but just the same, he's dead. I guess the difference is one of them was on my side. That's the main difference...but they were both killers.'

Michael said, 'don't think too deep Icy, you did the job. We didn't tell you how to do it so forget the morality shit. The hit was less important than the other stuff.'

Icy said it didn't sound much of a trade to lose Henry for an SS man but there was a lot more and he filled in the gaps. Michael had a face set in stone and acted serious. Icy knew he was thinking how to make things sound good with Mossad. They had a secure line to the embassy in New York where people waited to signal Tel Aviv but nobody was anxious to make the call yet.

'What you told us so far equals some dead people and not much else. Tel Aviv won't be happy with that.'

'Listen to the good news and smile, Michael. It took two years but we got the stuff.'

Michael asked how much there was and where. Icy said Michael was sitting on it and helped him out of the rocking chair. Icy said the chair was a work of art and the others looked impatient. Then he told them about a carpenter who ruled over Jews in the camps and what he did. They didn't recognise it was Gunter.

'Get it in your heads this guy was a serious trickster. The persons above you gotta understand this project was complicated.' Icy saw they lost focus.

Michael said, 'if you got something to show us...?'

Icy laid the rocking chair on its side then crossed to a drawer and took out a hammer and chisel. He tapped the chisel in where the chair's arm joined the front support and detached it. The joints were perfect, and didn't need glue. Next, he levered the arm away from the rear strut and when it was free showed it to them. There was still nothing to see. He went to the drawer, got some fine pincers and a linen cloth and told the expert to stand close. He spread the cloth on the floor and kneeled down holding the arm of the chair. Using the pincers, Icy teased a wedge of packing from the hollow centre of the arm. When he turned it vertical, diamonds cascaded out onto the linen cloth. Now they paid attention. The expert viewed a diamond with his eyepiece and said it was flawless.

Michael was not satisfied until every hollow piece of the rocking chair was detached and laid on the floor. The security men stopped Michael from smashing the wood. Icy told him it was made with great skill so there was no point but it sent him into a rage. Their expert separated the diamonds into piles while a security man phoned New York and told them what they'd found. The security man covered the mouthpiece and said Mossad needed all the parts of the chair shipped back to Israel and Michael calmed down.

Icy said, 'Mossad will put the wood through X-rays in Tel Aviv. They never trust field men because we ain't thorough like their scientists. I'll order coffee so take deep breaths until I come back, Michael.'

When he returned, the security man with the phone asked if there was a chance that documents were hidden somewhere in the chair. Icy said no because they'd seen everything when he broke it up in front of them. The expert who examined the diamonds told Michael they seemed perfect but it was impossible to value them until they were back in Israel. He put the stones into a diplomatic bag that he chained to his wrist. He was anxious to get moving and the security men took the parts of the chair with them when they left. Michael stayed behind.

'So that's it Michael and with a little time I can wash up the operation like it never existed.'

'It exists...things exist that should never have started but they exist. I wish those stones had been shown to anybody but me.' Michael was agitated and walked the length of the room, 'my mother liked diamonds and her and my aunts wore them when I was a kid...we were a rich family and people wore diamonds like you wear shoes. At night, the women wore necklaces and rings and we all laughed a lot. I was skinny in those days and remember how the women sparkled.'

'Cool down Michael. Try to forget until you got no option. With our operation we got a result.'

Michael finally sat in a vibrating chair at the end of the room and switched it on, but his fat was hardened by his soul and it didn't shake. Icy went over and switched off the motor when he saw Michael was crying.

'Diamonds do strange things but I never saw them upset a guy like this.'

'My folks paid to get me out of Germany with our family diamonds but they didn't manage to escape. After I was gone they gassed them all - mother, father, aunts and uncles. Maybe some of those stones were used to keep me alive,' Michael rubbed his eyes and his breath came in a shudder, 'it's OK Icy, I'm back with you. Let's wrap it up.'

He calmed down and said Tel Aviv asked what Icy wanted now because he was blown. They owed him. Icy said all he needed was some time for his face to heal and then back to the army in Israel.

'Take three months vacation. I can advance your salary.'

'Three months is fine to travel around Europe. Kinda sad for us two, but maybe it's time to quit.'

'Mossad has rules that say I can never be your controller again Icy. You know I'm sorry your boy was killed while you ran him, but things like that happen.'

'He was a great kid, Michael.'

40

New York City

Thursday 14.30 - 24th February 1966

The flight was late and Henry spent the morning getting familiar with the airport terminal. After lunch, he called Karl's number from a payphone and hung up when Karl answered. His luck was in and he stored his bag in left luggage. February in New York was a shock after Caribbean temperatures and the taxi driver turned up the heater for him. Icy had a rule in their world that said keep a safe house even your masters don't know about. Icy rented an apartment in a seedy block with a view of Brooklyn Bridge. Henry let himself in and checked the place. Dust was thick and undisturbed by visitors. He didn't plan to stay long and had a connecting flight in six hours but bolted the door anyway.

He found a paper knife amongst the dried-up pens in a desk. A single window let in weak light and looked out on the blank wall of another building. Henry pried a board free from the window alcove with the paper knife and laid it on the carpet. Two emergency bags tied with elastic sat in the recess below the panel. They were for him and Icy. Henry took one out, put back the panel, and banged it flush again. The .38-calibre revolver inside the bag was loaded and Henry checked the safety catch and slipped it into his jacket. He put the folded bag into another pocket then let himself out and locked the door.

New York's street grid system made it easy to find an address and Henry walked fast to keep warm. Karl's block was in a fashionable district with an elevator available but Henry walked up ten flights of stairs to the top floor. There was a fire escape onto the roof. Henry knocked on his apartment door and Karl opened it.

'Hey guy, you came to visit,' said Karl.

'You bet.'

'Come in,' said Karl with a smile.

'Sorry Gunter couldn't make it for his birthday,' Henry pulled the gun, 'let's talk on the roof.'

Karl knew about guns and walked out without closing the door. They went up the fire stair to an emergency exit. Karl was calm but the .38 nudged his spine as they went onto the roof. Henry told Karl to face him.

'What's this about?' said Karl.

'I got curious about Gunter and you and thought maybe you hung on to some interesting secrets.'

'Who're you working for?' said Karl.

'My boss likes to keep that private.'

'I had a boss like that.'

'What kind of boss?' Henry raised the gun.

'Russian guy called Akulov. He captured us in Russia and threatened to dig out Gunter's brain in front of me unless I kept him informed of stuff he needed. He demonstrated how it would happen on a Polish prisoner. After the war, he wanted to know our location. Couple of times I ducked out but each time he sent a reminder to keep me nervous. All those years, Gunter never knew I told this guy where he was. A few years back Gunter moved out to the Caribbean.'

'OK,' said Henry, and nudged Karl closer to the low wall that bordered the roof. A pigeon flew up from the shadows and Karl raised his arm to ward off the bird. Henry dropped into a firing position but relaxed when Karl put his arm down again.

'I have money. Let me go and it's yours...it's the only secret worth anything.'

'Keep talking.'

'At the side of the bed in my apartment is a cigarette box.'

'Yeah,' said Henry.

'The bottom is false and comes out if you use a knife. There's an envelope underneath.'

'So?'

'In the envelope is information about a numbered bank account with money deposited in it.'

'Where'd you get the money?' said Henry.

'Me and Gunter collected gold in the war and traded it for dollars.'

'Gold is hard to come by,' said Henry.

'Where we worked a lot of it got left by dead Jews. Only him and me know about the account.'

'Neat,' said Henry.

'Do we have a deal?'

'There's something more.'

'What?'

'Gunter is dead.'

Karl's face was pale and he seemed to choke. The pigeon landed on the wall and hopped cautiously towards its secret hideaway. It went behind Karl and flapped down into the shadows.

'Tell me it isn't true.'

'It's true,' said Henry, 'I killed him.'

'That sonofabitch gone and left me after all this time. I loved him like nobody else could. Gave him things since we were kids…looked after him sick or well. It's our birthday today and you go and tell me you killed him and he's dead. Oh, I loved him so much. You'll never understand why we shared the same birthday and now he's left me. He was supposed to ship a present to New York and meet for our birthday today,' Karl said. The wind moved debris around the roof and Karl's trousers flapped. He was white as the clouds that blew across the city sky behind him.

'So I'm not staying – you've killed us both. Gunter and me stick together,' he turned at a run and leaped from the back of the building ten floors high. The pigeon flew up from its haven and hovered for a second in the cold wind, then soared down as if to follow Karl.

Henry looked over the parapet and saw Karl's body lying in an alley at the rear of the block. Nobody seemed to have noticed and the alley was empty. He sprinted down the fire stair to the apartment and locked the door behind him. The cigarette box was on a table by the side of the bed and he took it to the kitchen and emptied cigarettes in the waste bin. Its false bottom came away with the help of a bread knife and the envelope was there as Karl promised. There were two sheets of paper inside. On the first was the name and address of a European bank and details of a numbered account. On the second was a balance statement and the account number matched the number on the first sheet. The figures showed a deposit of more than two million dollars. Access to the account was by number alone. Henry put both sheets in his jacket.

He took the paper bag from his pocket, wiped the gun clean and dropped it in the bag. There was no sound outside the apartment door. Henry checked the floor was empty and took the elevator to the ground floor. He flagged a taxi outside the main entrance of the apartment block and told his driver to turn up the heater.

After Henry paid off his driver at the airport he went to the men's rest room. When it was empty, he dropped the bag and gun into a trash bin and covered it with paper towels. He reclaimed his stuff from the luggage storage area in the concourse, checked in for a domestic flight then picked up a schedule from the desk of an international carrier. Henry flicked through the destinations. Icy's bonus money put him in funds for a leisurely trip to visit Karl's European bank.

*

41

The Caribbean - San Juan

Friday 12.00 - 25th February 1966

Icy's mood lifted when there was just him and his Haitian girl with her sketchbook and crayons. They didn't have much time left together but she was well provided for. She didn't know his plans and put ointment on the burn on his face. He told her to get some food together. Later they could walk round the old city in San Juan and maybe stand on the walls of El Morro fort.

While she was in the kitchen preparing their food, she sang in French and Icy locked the door. He went to the vibrating chair pushed against the wall at the far end of the room where Michael had sat and switched on the power. He reclined the chair and extended both foot supports until they hit the stops. The metal supports were hollow and Icy extracted a cardboard cylinder from each one with his pincers. They contained documents previously hidden in Gunter's rocking chair.

Icy took two documents from the first cylinder and flattened them on a table. The parchment was thick and wanted to roll back into shape. Mossad had trained Icy in financial transactions with genuine bearer bonds issued by European Banks and he understood their value. This pair guaranteed five million US dollars for the holder of each bond. Possession meant ownership of the sums of money stated on them, which totalled ten million dollars from two bonds plus twenty-five years of attached interest coupons.

In the second tube were four other documents and Icy flattened these on the table. They were written in German, embossed with a Swastika and dated 1941. There were identical signatures on each one and he spread out the four receipts intended for American corporations. Details of money and diamonds that should have been received by them in 1941 were on each paper. These were the only copies and must be priceless evidence for someone. When it came to international politics and blackmail, Icy guessed they were worth more than the diamonds and bonds. He replaced the sets of documents into their tubes, hid them in the chair's foot supports and worked the control so they were invisible again.

Icy unlocked the door to the kitchen where his girl was still singing. He asked if she wanted to go to the old city and stand on the walls of El Morro fort. She nodded and put their food in a bag. They went out past the chair at the end of the room and he turned out the lights.

*

42

1967 Israel

Icy was soon bored without Henry to control and went home before his leave in Europe was finished. The Israeli army was happy to welcome back a volunteer soldier. Nobody knew what might happen and things were tense. The Middle East was a tinderbox and Israel waited for it to ignite with its army on high alert. When war came, Icy didn't know it would last six days and be called The Six Day War. Nor did he know if diamonds stolen from European Jews by Nazis would finance it. But he did know that when fighting started, Israel's forces were unrelenting.

With unwitting irony, Captain Ignacy Czeberowski told his men that someone must have paid for their bullets. After the first airstrike against Egypt on Monday, June 5th the unit heard a radio broadcast describing Israel's strategy as *diamond hard*. Captain Icy said this was a diamond war and they were cutting edge soldiers. His men joked that Icy knew a lot about precious stones. He said they could joke and it was fine so long as they all got out of 1967 intact, to drink beer in Tel Aviv and tell their families about the war. If that happened, he would throw a party for them. He had no relatives so be sure to turn up.

On Wednesday, June 7th 1967, in Jerusalem, they started a battle called Ammunition Hill, fighting against Jordanian troops. Jewish soldiers hoped they might take the Western Wall without loss and Israeli casualties were low though Jordanian soldiers fought hard. But that battle was for a Jewish holy place and the Israeli soldiers were fearless. Advance was so fast that maintaining contact with his unit was difficult for Icy. He discovered ethnic areas were good places to hide and draw breath from the heat of battle. The Armenian quarter provided cover from heavy firing during the attack, and his unit spread out from there to charge the hill. None of them saw it happen but Icy was shot in the face by a heavy calibre bullet and killed that afternoon. Medics found his body when the battle was over. His bloodstained white hair and a dog tag confirmed it was Icy. He was buried within 24 hours.

It was unlucky that Icy was shot with a stray bullet. He was the only soldier killed in his unit and his men stood to attention at the Christian cemetery in Jerusalem while four of them shovelled earth over his grave. They chanted Jewish prayers because there was no family to mourn his death. One soldier said it was sad that a Polish Christian should die fighting in a battle for Jerusalem. Another said that was a good reason they must never forget him.

43

Jerusalem

Friday - 23rd February 1968

There were hippies everywhere but it was unusual to see a black girl and white man wandering around a Christian cemetery in Jerusalem. The man wore his hair in a ponytail long enough to brush his shoulder bag. She was ebony black with aquiline features and wore a full-length robe. They spoke in slow English and read each inscription carefully on the headstones. It took time with her strong French accent.

'Pray we find him soon Henry.'

'Nobody said what name they marked on the stone,' said Henry.

'Show me his big name,' Henry flipped his notebook open so she could read the printed name - IGNACY CZEBEROWSKI.

'There are many letters.'

'Icy for short. He was a little guy with a big name,' said Henry. They came to a place in the cemetery reserved for the dead with no money. It was overgrown and the stones were small with basic inscriptions. Henry went from stone to stone and scraped off the moss to see the lettering. At the back of the plot, bushes covered a gravestone and Henry pushed them back and cleaned off the name. Stenciled in black military ink on it was the name IGNACY CZEBEROWSKI. There was no indication it was the grave of a soldier but Henry knew who it was.

Henry said, 'I'm still your kid Icy. We started together and you've ended up alone in a grave. Funny thing, we met at the Bashoura cemetery in Beirut and your girl and me are going there. She wants to see where we got together. I told her we'd visit the bar at the Normandie Hotel and sit at our table. Maybe the barman is alive and they can talk in French. I hitched up with your girl from Haiti but she still talks all the time about you and those chairs. A guy in this cemetery looks after graves for money and we made a deal if I found yours. From now on, you get maximum treatment in flowers every week. Roses and orchids, when he can get them.'

'Keep well Icy,' she said and Henry smiled.

'Sometimes her English isn't just right. With your ear for languages you'll know that,' Henry said.

The girl wandered off while he made the grave tidy. Behind the stone was a scrub and Henry struggled to uproot it. He almost gave up but when it gave way, Henry saw an ammunition pouch propped at the base stencilled with Icy's name. Henry unbuttoned it and took out a puppet with its nose stained black. Henry replaced it in the pouch and put the whole thing in his shoulder bag.

Henry said, 'you hung on to Gretel for our anniversary Icy. It's two years since I hit Gunter, and you know that's when this lady turned up at the party. By the way, it wasn't me that shot Meath, it was Gunter. There was nobody on the mountain that day except Gunter and me and I didn't pull the trigger. It wasn't the right time to tell you after the hit but I made up for it now. Another thing, that guy Karl jumped from his roof and left us two million dollars so I retired as a hitter. And, how about the stuff you were after? Maybe somebody got lucky if you found it. I know you chased important things, but never said what. That's all the news Icy.'

*

44

1969 England

The Doctor stopped drinking after Italia gave birth. It happened because his hands shook when he held the new baby. A controller who lost an agent got time to think about alcohol because its unwritten rule meant the service retired him. The Doctor had lost his agent and he stayed at home with Italia's baby and brooded about Jayce. It was an emotional distraction that cut deep. Then Italia received letters from a Swiss law firm nominating her as trustee of an investment fund set up for her son. A partner wanted to discuss the details. Italia arranged an appointment and asked that her husband also attend the meeting and this was accepted. Monsieur Abati, the firm's senior partner, wanted to handle things personally because of the size of the bequest.

Monsieur Abati produced a passport and letter of authority from his firm and spoke in good English.

'My firm are to act as administrators for this fund and have given an undertaking of confidentiality. We can disclose the identity of the benefactor and nothing more.'

'Do I know this person?' said Italia.

'Perhaps,' said Monsieur Abati.

'And my wife's position?' said The Doctor.

'Is to accept or decline her role as trustee. If she accepts she becomes responsible for the distribution of income from the fund until her son is 21 years old, at which time he inherits the investment fund itself,' said Monsieur Abati.

'Go on,' said The Doctor.

'The fund is derived from bonds and interest coupons that have now matured. We have invested the principal amount in two American corporations that were specified by the benefactor. Presently, we can approve an annual income of two hundred thousand US dollars a year payable to your wife as trustee, on behalf of the child,' said Monsieur Abati.

'Who is the benefactor?' said Italia.

'Ignacy Czeberowski,' said Monsieur Abati.

'I don't know that name.'

'Nevertheless, do you accept for your son?'

Italia looked at The Doctor, 'yes.'

'Sign these documents and we can proceed,' said Monsieur Abati.

*

45

1970 England

The Doctor stayed sober and cherished the time he spent with Italia's son. They called him Henry Junior – HJ at nursery. HJ loved the sea and as a break from nursery they spent weekends at the coast where he could watch Atlantic waves pound the beach. His preferred seat to watch the ocean was on a swing. On that particular Saturday, their special world together was Italia pushing from behind and The Doctor in front. In the evening, after HJ went to bed, The Doctor and Italia sat on their balcony and watched the moon while a gale blew in.

'Italia.'

'Yes.'

'Tell me the truth about something that puzzles me.'

'The truth about...?'

'About eyes,' said The Doctor.

Italia giggled, 'go on.'

'What colour are your eyes?'

'Brown,' said Italia.

'Can you remember the colour of Henry's eyes...I mean HJ's father?'

'Brown, also.'

'And HJ's eyes?' said The Doctor.

'Wonderful blue.'

'Ah,' said The Doctor.

'Ah?'

'You know I'm a doctor?'

'Yes.'

'It's unusual for HJ to have blue eyes if Henry is his father. Not impossible, but a man and a woman with brown eyes usually have a brown eyed child,' said The Doctor.

'HJ is my son.'

The Doctor said gently, 'is Henry his father or another man with blue eyes?' Italia choked back a scream and The Doctor cursed his clumsy approach. She stood up and the Atlantic gale hit full on and threw her hair into a halo around her dark skin. Yet HJ's skin was pale and his eyes blue.

'Nothing changes because HJ is ours,' said The Doctor.

'Promise to forgive me?'

'Yes,' said The Doctor.

'Henry had many women so I bought dresses from Gunter's shop to keep him interested.'

'I know that.'

'Gunter was kind and let me try things,' said Italia, 'often I changed between the dress rails. One time Gunter came out of his workshop when I was naked and saw me.'

'But he liked men.'

'He pulled me to him,' said Italia.

'And?'

'I wanted him and he took me.'

'What happened then?'

'He gave me a dress and said, "Gretel told me I needed a real woman before dying."'

'Our son looks just like Gunter,' said The Doctor.

'I know that he does, but Gunter left HJ *nothing* more than his looks.'

Italia went to the bedroom when she heard the child cry.

The Doctor sat for a moment then made a decision after four years of denial. He went to the lounge, took out a package hidden under the debris inside his medical bag, and tore it open. It needed all his nerve to look in Jayce's wallet for the first time since the Caribbean. Even now, it had a few grains of sand inside. His mind wandered to the floating body and his courage choked but he emptied the wallet and went through the papers. There was nothing exceptional until he unfolded a memo written in German and addressed to Gunter.

Sie sind mit 150 Treffern an der Ostfront ein herausragender Scharfschütze. In Anerkennung Ihrer Fähigkeiten sind Sie hiermit dazu eingeladen, mit mir an einer Hirschjagd teilzunehmen. Der genaue Ort und die Zeit werden Ihnen mitgeteilt, sobald wir Ihre Zustimmung erhalten haben.
Herzlichen Glückwunsch.

Heinrich Himmler

Scribbled at the bottom in English was written, *"It takes nerve for an outstanding sharpshooter with 150 hits on the eastern front to turn-down an invitation from The Reichsführer-SS, to hunt stag like you did."* **Karl**

Gunter killed Jayce because he stole Himmler's invitation to hunt stag. Jayce paid with his life and immortalised himself as sharpshooter hit number 151. The Doctor finally accepted who shot his nephew.

The Doctor watched the gale subside until Italia came out and handed HJ to him.

'Take him on the balcony for a while and the air will calm him,' and she went back to the bedroom. Within a minute HJ was fast asleep.

The Doctor touched HJ's cheek and whispered, 'every second we're together, your face will remind me your father murdered my nephew. And every other second it will remind me I saved your father's killer. Doctor Faustus put it well. Hell has no limits.'

46

Author's Comments

The Orphan Sniper is a work of fiction but the story is about real people and events. The character of Gunter is founded on a former SS concentration camp guard the author met in the Caribbean and who vanished in mysterious circumstances. Meath and Gelson are two crooks who sank boats for insurance purposes.

Icy and Henry are characters the author met in Beirut and perhaps, like Gunter they created their own fiction. They came and went during drinking sessions in Jackie Mann's bar long before Palestinian fighters took Jackie hostage.

Fritz, the briefing officer in 1941, has an interesting connection. He also is fictitious but the author used a genuine SS officer, Fritz Darges, for his character. Adolph Hitler dismissed Darges for impertinence two days before the Valkyrie assassination attempt and sent him to the Russian front. Had he stayed, Darges would probably have died in the bomb blast. At the time of writing, Fritz Darges was in his nineties and still alive in Germany - he is now dead.

In 1945, liberators arrested Hjalmar Schacht in the Tyrol following transfer from Dachau concentration camp. He faced trial for war crimes at

Nuremberg and was one of only three senior Nazis acquitted. Mr Justice Jackson, the American prosecutor was outraged and branded Schacht as...*the most dangerous and reprehensible type of all opportunists, someone who would use Hitler for his own ends.* Shortly afterwards Justice Jackson was prematurely recalled to the United States. Schacht prospered as a banker and died in 1970 at the age of 93.

In the spring of 1945, Himmler sanctioned the release of over 7,000 women from Ravensbrück Concentration Camp into the hands of the Swedish Red Cross. Some men accompanied them.

Aircraft that flew the pre-emptive Israeli strike in the 1967 Six Day War were mostly French built and paid for by Israel herself. After that war, the USA became a proactive financier and today the Israeli Air Force is mainly equipped with American and Israeli aircraft.

Details of the opening of The Queen Elizabeth Bridge are factual and Buckingham Palace provided the itinerary. The place where the sting took place is Bellamy Cay in The British Virgin Islands. It is now a restaurant called *The Last Resort*.

The two American corporations with financial interests in Germany during WW2 are fictitious. The USA did not enter WW2 until December 1941 though allegedly, some US companies had continued trading with Nazi Germany. At the end of the war there was no evidence produced to show that any of those companies received profits.

Printed in Great Britain
by Amazon.co.uk, Ltd.,
Marston Gate.